'The coronation of Charles the Great on Christmas Day in the year 800 was the central event of the middle ages, and altered the history of the world.' One of the sets of his regalia is the subject of *Grave Goods*.

Tamara Hoyland, the clever, cool, intrepid heroine of Jessica Mann's earlier novels, finds that a man seems to be trying to kill a woman called Margot Ellice. Only one thing about Margot Ellice is especially interesting. She is writing about the life of the morganatic wife of the Prince of Horn in the mid-nineteenth century; the material is the correspondence between her, the former Lady Artemis Bessemer, and her sister Lady Clementine, written from the Horn family palaces and castles in East Prussia. Margot's book starts:

Lady Artemis Bessemer was sold by her father to the Hereditary Prince of Horn in the autumn of 1858.

Now an exhibition is to come to London from what was East Prussia – a diplomatic gesture on the part of the East Germans. The centrepiece will be the regalia of Charlemagne, which is thought never to have left the castle of the Princes of Horn at Drachenschloss before. But Margot Ellice, doing her historical research into earlier events at Drachenschloss, seems to have aroused many passions, from greed to embarrassment and terror. She will not be the only person to die as desperate attempts are made to cover up what really happened to those Carolingian treasures.

Tamara is faced with a complex puzzle, but she is at her most impressive in this new adventure, as is Jessica Mann, who has constructed a story of formidable virtuosity, lucidly and elegantly told, and leading to a fine ironic climax.

by the same author

A CHARITABLE END
MRS KNOX'S PROFESSION
THE ONLY SECURITY
THE STICKING PLACE
CAPTIVE AUDIENCE
THE EIGHTH DEADLY SIN
THE STING OF DEATH
FUNERAL SITES
NO MAN'S ISLAND

non-fiction

DEADLIER THAN THE MALE

JESSICA MANN
GRAVE GOODS

M
MACMILLAN

ISBN: 0 333 37973 X

First published 1984 by
MACMILLAN LONDON LIMITED
London and Basingstoke
Associated companies in Auckland Dallas Delhi
Dublin Hong Kong Johannesburg Lagos Manzini
Melbourne Nairobi New York Singapore Tokyo
Washington and Zaria

Typeset in Great Britain by
WILMASET
Birkenhead, Merseyside

Printed and bound in Great Britain by
ANCHOR BRENDON LIMITED
Tiptree, Essex

I

Blood was dripping from a cut on Margot Ellice's forehead onto her attacker's left hand, which was pressed over her nose and mouth. The man held an open clasp knife in his gloved right hand. Tamara Hoyland moved silently forward from the open doorway behind him, and chopped the side of her metal briefcase against his wrist. The knife clattered to the floor, and the man let go his hold of Margot Ellice, who slumped onto the sofa, gasping and moaning.

As the man whirled to face her, Tamara kicked the knife away. A glance showed her a face masked by brown nylon above a tall, muscular body in jeans, sweat shirt and anorak, with a sheaf of paper folded into the anorak pocket. His right hand hung uselessly. Through the stocking Tamara could see the movements of the man's eyes, but his quarrel, if he had one, was apparently not with her. He dashed for the door and was down the one flight of stairs and out into the street before Tamara had finished dialling the three slow numbers.

The police found no witness prepared to admit seeing him, and the old block of flats had not been attended by a porter since the war. Bloodstained rubber gloves and a ruined stocking were found at the bottom of the lift shaft.

Margot Ellice had thirteen stitches in the wound in her head and was kept in hospital overnight. Her employer and charge, Tamara's bedridden grandfather, had heard nothing and was not told of the intruder into the apartment that had been his home for fifty years. Tamara's mother, his only daughter, took unpaid leave from her work as a producer of schools' radio programmes, to take care of him.

II

Lady Artemis Bessemer was sold by her father to the Hereditary Prince of Horn in the autumn of 1858.

A good first line. Margot Ellice read it aloud again, watching the girl's face. It would take an imaginative leap on her part to believe that Artemis could have been literally unfree. Written all over Tamara Hoyland's appearance was the label of her generation: a free woman, bound by no other individual, never trained to submit, or tend, or defer.

Twenty years younger than I am, Margot thought, and a different species. I have more in common with poor Artemis than with this creature of liberty.

Tamara Hoyland, who had come sick visiting, said, 'She sounds rather a spiritless girl, your heroine.'

'Unlike you,' Jeremy Ellice said. He had brought Tamara down to the basement room, usually his own all-purpose sanctum, where he had installed his sister when she was discharged by the hospital. He was sitting on the end of the bed leafing through the evening paper. 'There's nothing in here about your spirited intervention on Margot's behalf, Tamara.'

'I should hope not,' Tamara said.

She takes that kind of thing for granted, Margot thought. In the world she has inherited it is natural for a girl to defend herself or her friends. No man would dare to attack her in the first place. Margot's husband had assaulted her many times during the long years of her marriage, and had controlled her movements and her behaviour. Now that it was over, she could not be sure whether she had wasted so many miserable years serving him and nursing his odious and disgusting mother from fear, or from the residual sense of natural duty that her upbringing and education had inculcated.

'I suppose a poor thing like Artemis Bessemer is unimaginable to you,' Margot told Tamara.

'Did she have to let herself be sold like a slave?'

Jeremy was still reading aloud nuggets from the evening paper. 'Treasures never before seen in the West go on show this weekend in London. This exhibition is the first of its kind to come from East Germany since the war.'

'Artemis Bessemer had to live in Germany,' Margot said.

Tamara asked, 'Couldn't she have run away? Or even said she did *not* take this man to be her wedded husband?'

'That's what comes next,' Margot said.

It has to be understood that Artemis had literally no choice in the matter. She was as much at her father's disposal as any of his chattels; his was both the power and the legal right to dispose of her. Nor did his behaviour seem especially deplorable to his contemporaries, for marriages were counters of trade and bargain, in which the preferences of the two parties might be of greater or lesser weight. Artemis's father himself had made a businesslike marriage to the only child of a commoner who had made a fortune in India and come home to buy a title for himself and an Earl for his daughter. Neither the nabob nor Lady Bessemer had lived to see the final dissipation of that wealth. The Earl of Bessemer was in no

8

position to provide a dowry for either of his daughters and was delighted when Joachim von Horn offered good money in exchange for one of them.

It was a *mésalliance*. The penniless granddaughter of the nabob was not of equal rank with the Prince of Horn, even though on her father's side she descended from the Plantagenet kings. She could not display the complete number of quarterings on her arms to satisfy the requirements of the higher German nobility for a 'full and perfect marriage'. The Prince was willing to make a 'left-handed' marriage, what the English called morganatic. It was fully binding in that neither party was free to marry anyone else, and their children would be legitimate but without the right of succession to their father's titles or entailed properties. Prince Joachim was twenty-eight and believed that this rule, along with many others, would be altered in his lifetime. The diarist Lutwige, who was staying in London at the time, recorded that the Prince declared to the Earl of Bessemer that he would not submit to mediaeval restrictions, and would help his countrymen to cast off similar shackles.

Lord Bessemer was not interested in reform. He wanted the tangible reward. There is no reason to suppose that either man felt the least remorse. The Queen deplored their bargain. She wrote to her sister, Princess Feodore of Hohenlohe Langenburg, herself the wife of a German princeling, of 'this CRUEL custom, that a *lady* who is eligible to marry ANY English nobleman is INSULTED by such treatment in Germany.' During her life Queen Victoria was to record many disapproving remarks about morganatic marriages. She did not comment, however, on the businesslike nature of the transaction. The Queen's own daughter, Vicky, was shortly to make a blatantly political alliance with Prince Frederick William of Prussia, but Vicky and Fritz obediently loved each other. They had known for several years that it was their duty to do so.

The Prince Consort remonstrated with the Earl of Bessemer when they met at a banquet in the City of London. To Lord Bessemer Prince Albert was nothing but a foreign upstart.

9

He replied with neither deference nor obedience, 'My daughter's affairs, sir, are not your Royal Highness's, but mine.'

The Queen wrote indignantly, 'Dearest Albert was addressed most *disrespectfully* by Ld. Bessemer, whom I have always DISLIKED.' However, for the sake of the late Dowager Lady Bessemer, who was popular at court when Victoria was young, Artemis was kindly received at her presentations just before, and again just after, her marriage, which took place a few weeks before that of the Princess Royal and her Fritz. The Queen told Artemis that her English face would be welcome at the Prussian court, and noted in her diary, 'The Prince of Horn has been wild in his youth, but the GOOD INFLUENCE of an *English* Lady will have wonderful results.'

Artemis Bessemer was eighteen years old. Her fate had been precipitated by her having been so bold as to peep, and so rash as to be seen peeping, at the procession of guests on their way into dinner at Bessemer House in Belgrave Square.

It is natural to stare at princes. When Joachim looked up and saw Artemis doing so through the balustrade of the staircase, she thought no more than that she had been detected in a breach of manners. She curtseyed and backed away. Although she had seldom met or even seen young men, Joachim made little impression, for he is not mentioned in her journal, but for him it was love, or perhaps desire, at first sight.

Artemis and Clementine Bessemer had been brought up in Devonshire by their governess, a Mrs Lambert, a Prussian who had met, married and soon mourned a young English diplomat called Edwin Lambert. No flash of the charm that had captivated him in Berlin was visible when the young widow applied to become the governess of Lady Bessemer's daughters. Nor did Lady Bessemer see, in the dowdy mouse before her, a woman who was capable of teaching her charges much more than the superficial accomplishments required by an upper class lady. But during their isolated years in the country, Artemis and Clementine became better educated than most of their contemporaries. They were grounded in Latin and Greek and classical mythology, in French and German, and in the natural sciences. They learnt little about

10

religion, and took as their childish totem the goddess Artemis, or Diana, whose statue stood in an elegant grotto at Stockwell, their home in Devon. In their childhood journals, both girls mention the offerings that they made to her, and the treasures they hid inside the stone plinth on which she stood. They also took an informed interest in politics. Mrs Lambert's own views, which would have disqualified her from employment in any genteel household if she had admitted to them, were agnostic and revolutionary; she disapproved of monarchy, and dreaded autocracy.

All the same, Mrs Lambert knew that the Earl of Bessemer had the legal right to be an autocrat to his own children. They were careful to keep their true thoughts from him, and must have hidden their journals too. Clementine's diary of those years survived in a trunk full of her papers. It is detailed and literate, and includes much abstract musing, perhaps because there were few events to record. Only once is any man other than the Earl himself and the village parson mentioned, when Mrs Lambert's brother from Germany came to visit her. The two girls were not permitted to meet him but spied from behind hedges and walls as he walked with his sister. He was a tall man, with brown hair and eyes and very white teeth, Clementine wrote. When the girls asked Mrs Lambert to talk about him, she set an essay on the subject of Henry VIII instead. That Sunday, Artemis scandalised the Vicar by saying that the established church was the result of that King's unbridled urges, and the Vicar said he would complain to the Earl. The girls' intellectual awareness was not balanced by worldly knowledge, which, as it turned out, might have been of more use.

They knew so little, in fact, that Artemis imagined it was worth trying to escape the fate her father had settled for her. If she had succeeded in running away, she might have ended up as a prostitute or a kitchen maid. The only work available to a lady, as a governess, would not have come her way. No employer would have taken on a girl who was young, beautiful and without references. Perhaps it was as well that her attempt at flight ended at the Great Western Railway Station, where

11

she was trying to buy a ticket to Exeter with money that Mrs Lambert had lent her.

Lord Bessemer sent Mrs Lambert and Clementine straight back to Devon. Without their company, Artemis was married in the private chapel at Belgrave Square to the Prince of Horn.

Artemis von Horn was photographed before she left London, and painted after her marriage. One portrait still hangs in a German museum. She had a long face with high, wide cheek bones, a sharply pointed chin and semi-circular eyes, that are shown so violet-blue as to seem idealised; her golden hair has a pinkish tinge, her curved lips an expression of quizzical amusement. One can see, a century later, that if such a thing as love at first sight exists, it might be for a girl who looked like this.

Prince Joachim paid for the trousseau, which included clothes of a kind that Artemis had never seen or imagined; maids and lady attendants arrived from Germany, and all that she could provide in return, as her father made clear, was her own compliant person. Even she could see why she was expected to think herself lucky.

III

'Of course it's a first draft,' Margot Ellice said. 'I wrote it like this to get everything straight in my mind. It's meant to be an experiment in biography, like *The Quest for Corvo*. Narrative alternated with dramatic dialogue and quotations from my sources. I still have a lot of work to do, but I don't feel up to it at the moment.' Margot fingered the bandage swathing her head with a deprecatory finger, twitching her scabbed lips into as much of a smile as she could simulate.

'The poor girl is still addled,' Jeremy Ellice said.

'I'm not surprised,' Tamara commented.

'But it's better today, isn't it Margot?' Jem said.

Margot shrugged and said, 'Time heals all wounds, I'm told.'

'They said it wouldn't leave a scar,' Jeremy told Tamara.

'Do they seem any closer to finding out who—?'

'I don't think they are even trying!' Margot exclaimed. 'So many people get mugged and robbed in central London, they go through the fingerprint and question process as though it was a meaningless ritual. They said I was lucky to get off so lightly.'

'And your grandfather too,' Jeremy Ellice said.

'I feel bad about leaving him in the lurch,' Margot said.

'My mother is looking after him,' Tamara said.

'How can she get away? Her own work –'

'She's had to take unpaid leave.'

'Surely there's someone else?'

'It isn't easy, we are all so busy. I have had more than my leave allowance this year, my sister's got the children to look after, my brother's abroad . . . not that we'd be any good at it anyway. I don't think my mother is either. Even if one has the inclination to care for the bedridden it takes a certain amount of skill – well, Margot, you'd know that.'

The subject was a touchy one; Margot had spent her married life looking after her own disagreeable mother-in-law, and as soon as her services as an unpaid nurse and skivvy were not needed her husband had traded her in for a Mark II wife half her age. Her experience with caring for the old had made her a suitable choice of attendant for the old Count Losinsky, and she had needed a roof over her head and a salary at the time; but there was no suggestion that it was the type of work Margot Ellice would ever have chosen. Her childhood ambition had been to be a woman don. 'She's lucky to get the job,' Jeremy Ellice had unfeelingly told the Hoylands, but they felt a guilty unease at exploiting her need.

Tamara looked at Margot's grey, powdery face and the stitched wound left exposed to heal on her forehead. 'I still don't know what actually happened, Margot. How did that man get into the flat? Had he forced his way in?'

'He must have, I suppose. He was there when I got back from buying some food.'

'What, you came upon him in the flat? How horrible for you.'

'He was standing at the desk. It looked as though he

14

was going through my papers. I was so silly – one doesn't expect that kind of thing, after all – I must have subconsciously assumed he was someone with a right to be there. I said something ridiculous, good morning or something like that, and . . . .'

'He jumped you?'

'Yes. And then you arrived.'

'I hope the household insurance will cover your stuff,' Tamara said.

'I had nothing valuable anyway. No jewellery or anything. The man had some of my papers in his hand when I came in, he probably got away with those . . . it's funny though.'

'What?'

'It almost looked as though he was searching for something in particular. It can't possibly be true, I have nothing anyone could want to search for . . . I'm imagining it.'

'It certainly doesn't sound like the usual sneak thief.'

'Anyway, what could anyone want my old letters and bills for? He'd be welcome to them. The only thing I'd really be sorry to lose is the material I'm using for this book, and that's all here at Jem's place.'

'I am sorry the man got away with anything at all.'

'He might have got away with my life if it hadn't been for you, Tamara.'

'Look what I found for you,' Jeremy said. 'Several of the books on your list. Here's the *Reminiscences of Court and Diplomatic Life*, by Lady Bloomfield, and the *Letters of Lady Augusta Stanley*, and the memoirs of some unpronounceable Prussian Princess. And I thought you might like something lighter to cheer you up, so I bought in a batch of thrillers.'

'It will take more than that to . . . I don't know when I'll feel . . .'

15

'Feeling rotten? We'll leave you to have a sleep,' Jeremy said.

'No, wait, listen, Tamara, I want you to take the file with you, I want to know what you think, just the first part . . .'

'It's very good,' Jeremy said. 'I read it all yesterday.'

'I am not an historian, Margot, I'm an archaeologist,' Tamara said.

'Yes, yes, I know that, but you are a contemporary example of the type of woman I'm writing about, the woman who would have been at a man's mercy a hundred years ago. A graduate. High up in the Civil Service –'

'Not all that high.'

'And self supporting, and making your own decisions – if you'd been born when Artemis Bessemer was you'd have been a chattel so long as your father or husband was alive and destitute without them. You'd have had to go into some sort of service. I did myself, in a way, a century later. Now Artemis, you see, she's merely an example. I'm using her life story as an epitome. It doesn't matter whether she lived in a cottage or a castle. Here we have the raw material of history, this unique contemporary evidence . . .' Margot waved her bandaged hand with undirected energy.

Her brother picked up the cardboard folder and said, 'That's right, old girl. Tamara can read this later and you can discuss it then.'

'I shall give you the second half tomorrow. When I've made some corrections. It tells an extraordinary story, you'll be astonished, Tamara. You, specially, I can't wait to see your reactions. What I've got in here . . .' Margot stroked the second cardboard folder with creative pride.

'Leave it now, Margot, get some rest,' Jeremy Ellice

16

said. Tamara followed him out of the room. Outside its enclosure of warm light and multi-coloured draperies, the house changed in character. 'I live in one room,' Jeremy had explained when Tamara arrived with her flowers and good wishes, and he had taken her down to the basement of a house that was otherwise entirely full of books.

The only external sign that this tall terraced house in Hampstead was a bookshop, was a tiny plaque beside the front door bell, on which were inscribed the just legible words, *Jeremy Ellice, Reg. Office*. Customers who wanted to call in person made appointments, but most of Jeremy's business was done by mail. A box of newly printed catalogues was obstructing the entrance hall, and all the other passages were narrowed by heaps of books; volumes stacked on each step left six inches footway up the stairs. On coming in, Tamara had heard Margot's faint voice calling, 'Is that Tamara Hoyland? Do bring her down at once,' and had not stopped. Now, ascending to the ground floor, Jeremy said, Would you like to look round?' and Tamara eagerly agreed.

'Nothing I like better than a really jumbled second hand bookshop. But are you sure you don't mind?'

'Of course not, the shop's open for business.' He flicked on a row of light switches, illuminating the book-lined stair well. 'Take your time.'

Archaeological books were on the first floor, along with history, art history and natural history. Tamara prowled enviously along the rows of publications that cannot have seemed cheap when they were new and were now quite beyond the means of a working archaeologist like herself. The books she bought were more often those she did not really need and the second and attic floors contained a tempting range of them. What must have been the master bedroom was full of cookery books,

17

gardening guides, and a vast selection of self-improve-ment manuals, from the advice on etiquette of the last century, to more modern self-expression. The back room, still with its nursery bars over the window, was lined and piled with fiction. Tamara leafed through forgotten volumes by long ignored writers, wondering whether their time had been well spent; yet she could imagine the unalloyed delight of holding a novel with her own name on the spine, and had an undefined, not entirely logical notion that producing one would, in some way, justify her existence. So far, when story telling had twitched at her mind, she had pushed the thought away. One could understand the purpose of archaeology. What good would the outpourings of her personal subconscious be either to readers, or to herself?

For the time being, Tamara read, borrowed and bought fiction, and here was a treasure house of it; she picked out a couple of early thrillers, a first edition of one of Rebecca West's novels, a cookery book, a detective story by Glyn Daniel and one of C. P. Snow's *Strangers and Brothers* series.

'You chose the ones that have professional connections I see,' Jeremy Ellice remarked. 'An archaeologist, a civil servant, and a free woman.'

'I get ideas from them.'

'What ideas do you get from John Buchan? This one is a spy story I think.'

'Various tips, here and there.'

'I doubt whether one could use fiction as a recipe,' Jem said, wrapping her up a copy of Dorothy Hartley's *Food in England*. 'Not like this one.'

'That is for when I'm marooned on a desert island. It explains how to do everything from scratch.'

'You look as though you would be resourceful enough without instruction. I still have to thank you for rescuing

18

my sister. Where did you learn to cope as you did? Most girls would have fled screaming. And you look so fragile.'

'I really didn't do much.'

'That isn't what Margot told me. She said that you laid into the man like an Amazon.'

'I suppose I lost my temper.'

'That was either foolhardy or brave, then. But I can't think how you managed to fight off a man Margot described as a thug. You're a redoubtable girl.'

Somehow the bleak and shop-like ground floor had been transformed while Tamara was upstairs into a cosy room, like a cave turned into a home. Jem Ellice had aimed the spotlights to illuminate the rich leather covers of his most valuable wares, and had erected two wooden garden chairs, with brightly striped seats, on either side of the old fireplace, in which a gas fire hissed its blue flames. The mantelpiece carried a large black marble clock, with pillars supporting a triangular pediment. Miniature books were stacked between the pillars. Beside the hearth a mahogany table held heaps of literary publications, the *London* and *New York Review of Books*, *The Times Literary Supplement*, the *Bookseller*, *Encounter*, stacked beside various specialist journals of which Tamara had never heard.

'It's awfully nice here,' Tamara said.

'Sit down while I fetch some tea.'

'I'll get on with your sister's manuscript. She's sure to ask me what I think of it.'

19

IV

The wedding of the Prince of Horn and Lady Artemis Bessemer took place eight weeks before that of the Princess Royal and Prince Frederick William of Prussia. The two royalties had been chaperoned by a furiously bored Queen throughout a season of drawing room chats at Osborne and gentle walks at Balmoral. They were never alone together, but it was conventionally accepted that they were in mutual spontaneous love.

Artemis Bessemer was in Prince Joachim's company twice; once when she refused to marry this stranger, again when she was united to him.

The Princess Royal took her leave of her home in the presence of a crowd shouting, 'Be good to her or we'll have her back.' She and the Prince Consort clutched each other in tearful embraces before he left her in the cabin of the royal yacht.

The Earl of Bessemer said a curt goodbye to his daughter at the steps of the house in Belgrave Square before walking off to his club, relief marked in every line of his body. Artemis and Joachim von Horn set off, accompanied by their German attendants, in a procession of coaches. Artemis wrote to Clementine:

I am resolved to learn to respect my husband, and to make a life that I shall be able to share with you, dear sister, for I shall send for you, and for our dear Mrs Lambert, as soon as I may.

Mrs Lambert had written to Artemis that the Prince surely would be kind, though she might be surprised at some of his demands. 'He will expect obedience,' Mrs Lambert warned.

Unlike the Princess Royal, to whom tears came as easily as practised smiles, Artemis was determined not to cry. She reminded herself of French aristocrats going to the guillotine with gallantry, of Royalist heroines refusing to give their family secrets to Cromwell's men. Artemis and Clementine had acted out many heroic roles. She promised, 'He shall not see me tremble.'

Prince Joachim spoke little on the way to Gravesend. Once he touched her hand and said, 'I shall make you happy. In Germany we expect love to follow marriage, not precede it.'

After all, there were many things to make a girl happy. The thirteenth Hereditary Prince of Horn and Reiss and Drachensfeld (to abbreviate his full title) was among the richest men in Europe. He was the head of a famous, if now impotent, princely house, a Count of the Holy Roman Empire, a Baron of this, Lord of that – his description in the marriage contract had covered half a sheet of parchment. Artemis was to have jewels, money, furs, hunters, carriages, ladies-in-waiting. What lay ahead sounded dazzling in comparison with the schoolroom in Devonshire.

Artemis was the only one of the party not to suffer during the crossing from Gravesend to Antwerp. Joachim and all the servants were prostrated, and Artemis paced the deck alone. It was the last time she would be alone for a long time. Her ladies-in-waiting said, 'The wives of princes are always accompanied. It is not done to be unattended.'

I am learning of many things that are not done, Artemis wrote. It was not done for husbands and wives to travel in the same carriage, even on a wedding journey. Artemis was attended by her two ladies, Frau von Brucke, the widow of a Baron, who frequently mentioned her husband's rank, and Fräulein von Lansdorf, whose late father had been a general. Both treated Artemis with distant ceremony, and although they shared her travelling conveyances neither would sit down in her presence when they stopped at inns. It was not done. However, along with the deference to her husband's rank, Artemis recognised their scorn for a wife who was not well enough born to share it.

21

They curtseyed to her, but derisively, she thought.

The inns they stopped at were appalling. The servants hastened to lay the beds and tables with Joachim's own linen and silver and to spread his own carpets on the rough board floors, but the heating was inadequate, the furniture primitive, and every night there were fleas and bed bugs. It was not done for Artemis to wear day clothes for dinner. She was obliged to put on the low cut dresses provided in her trousseau, revealing skin bumpy from insect bites. It was not done to wear a shawl.

Artemis had not known that married people were expected to share the same room, let alone the same bed. She was astonished when Joachim entered at one door and the maids simultaneously left by the other. Naturally she did not write of her experiences. It is from later veiled references after her child was born that one can deduce her reactions. She wrote then of the stupidity of hiding all information from the young, and of the shock it is to a girl to discover by experience things of which she could have been forewarned. *For very few men is love what a young girl supposes it to be*, she concluded.

Yet there can be no doubt that Joachim von Horn did love Artemis. Only a powerful emotion could have made him flout the rules of his caste by marrying out of it, and although money meant little to him, he had paid a lot for her. His definition of love, however, could hardly match Artemis's. To a romantic girl of the eighteen fifties, love meant the meeting of two minds; to Joachim, of two bodies, and ungently at that. His name, like the Earl of Bessemer's, appears on the list of a well known brothel in London's Soho, which specialised in providing young virgins, often bound or even chloroformed, for its clients. Many outwardly respectable men of the period were regular customers of such establishments; Joachim was not unusual. Artemis was unusual in that she was able to work out a logical explanation of what was happening. She had learnt something of physiology in her unconventional education, and she had seen what animals did, though it took her a while to draw the analogy. She reached a conclusion that, if neither complete nor correct, enabled her to understand that Joachim's actions had not been the aberration of an abnormal

22

man but the common behaviour of all men.

At the time, Artemis did not write of this, or of anything concerning her husband; only her later letters give some clues about these early days of her married life.

The journey was long and boring. The ladies-in-waiting talked about clothes and people. It was not done, or they were not able, to speak of public affairs, or of the countries through which they travelled, or even of the landscape. Conversation was of the Princess this, or the Countess that, and their marriages, ancestors and appearance. The ladies could or would not play the few games that Artemis had brought in her luggage, or even read. *I am not fully persuaded that Frau von Brucke is able to read*, she told Clementine.

Once Artemis mentioned Mrs Lambert. 'She is a Prussian herself. It is she who taught me to speak German.'

'The English accent is not attractive in our language. You must allow me to correct you,' Fräulein von Lansdorf said. Artemis asked whether either lady might have known Mrs Lambert in Berlin.

'We do not know those who are not of the nobility.' That was definitely not done.

It was done to speak of the princely family with fawning expressions of esteem. Artemis would meet Prince Joachim's mother, the Princess Bathildis, his brother, Prince Waldemar, whose wife, Princess Ulrike, was a lady of great rank whose alliance had done honour to both houses, and numerous aunts and cousins who lived with the family. All were described as gracious, condescending, kind, beautiful and noble.

Joachim himself spoke to Artemis only when they met at the dinner table – in monologue. 'It is not done for ladies to express opinions on public affairs.'

This prince who had dared to marry a woman who could not be the mother of an heir, turned out, not surprisingly, to have reforming ideas about his own and his country's future, some of which he explained to Artemis. He had been a student in 1848, a 'year of terror' throughout Europe, when thrones tottered, and those who remembered the French Revolution feared (or hoped) that the mobs would triumph again.

Joachim had no wish to lose his throne, but he realised, more clearly perhaps than most German noblemen, how little power went with its pomp, and hoped to see some political realism introduced into the thinking of his class. Had his brethren known his thoughts they would have called him a dangerous radical. 'But we shall see reforms,' he assured his wife. 'When Prince Fritz is King, he will dedicate Prussia to the welfare of the people – the whole German people. We shall see many changes during our lifetime. And one of them will be the freeing of such princes as myself from the chains that fetter their choice of a bride. You shall be the reigning princess, and our son will inherit my titles and fortune.'

At present, as her ladies repeatedly made clear to Artemis, Prince Waldemar stood to inherit everything. Waldemar and Ulrike had a son and a daughter. 'She, of course, is eligible to marry the son of a king. Prince Joachim's children however . . .' Frau von Brucke had an habitual, sharp shrug with which she emphasised her denigratory remarks. She made it clear that she thought herself hard done by, having been reduced to waiting upon a lady who was not high-and-well-born, and on the day of their arrival at Horn itself she supervised the maids, as they dressed Artemis, with the expression of somebody who has been insulted.

The entourage consisted of numerous vehicles and outriders. For this last part of the journey Joachim sat beside Artemis in an open carriage. He wore uniform. Artemis had been put into a thin, low-cut dress, and her hair was coiled painfully around her head. She shivered with terror and cold as they crossed those last sandy miles of flat land. The Palace of Horn could be seen from far away. It was an immense white building, whose wings were spread across acres of land. Ranks of men in uniform or livery were lining the road, and stood in formation outside the Palace. At the foot of the curved staircase that led to the front door the Major Domo was waiting, and Joachim and Artemis followed him through the door, up the forty-five steps of the internal staircase, on each of which a footman stood, to the first floor, where rows of maids stood waiting to curtsey in unison at the Prince's approach.

24

The footmen wore blue coats covered with silver lace, with white gloves and gaiters. The maids wore short red dresses, with white fichus, aprons and stockings, and they had plaits of hair down their backs. The Major Domo was weighted down with gold braid.

Artemis noticed that the servants stared at her as though she were not a girl, but an example of some alien and unattractive species brought back from the Prince's travels for his menagerie. Somewhere the word 'Englishwoman' was being whispered.

The Major Domo walked backwards before them as they processed through five large reception rooms, each furnished with the spindly gold furniture that had been fashionable in England half a century earlier. All the walls were riotously frescoed; the pillars, mantelpieces and floors were made of multi-coloured marble. At their approach, footmen opened each pair of doors with practised unison. Artemis was to learn that all the servants, male and female, took part in a military style drill every day.

Joachim's family was assembled in the sixth salon. The Major Domo bawled out all his names and titles. Artemis, who had no right as a morganatic wife to her husband's rank, was not announced by name.

The princely family was grouped around a porcelain stove; a young man, taller and more handsome than Joachim, in similar uniform, and, like Joachim, with his chest covered with medals and orders: Prince Waldemar; their mother, seated beside Princess Ulrike and three other ladies, all immensely tall and stout, their bosoms protruding like shelves before them; an aunt, a cousin. Artemis curtseyed several times, with no acknowledgement. Several ladies stood silently against the walls, but none was presented, and Baroness von Brucke and Fräulein Lansdorf moved to join them.

Joachim drew Artemis closer to his relations, and his mother held out two fingers, which Artemis brushed with her lips.

After a while, Princess Bathildis said, 'She is very thin,' and another lady said, 'The English are always too thin.'

Artemis reported to Clementine that it was perhaps the

most uncomfortable half hour she had yet experienced. *None of the ladies addressed me. Perhaps they think I speak no German. They merely stared so that I did not know where to look. My husband and his brother left the room very soon, and it seemed an eternity before my new mamma crooked her finger at one of her ladies and said that I was to be shown to my apartments.*

Clementine wrote back that Artemis must ensure that she was treated as the mistress in her husband's house, a counsel of inexperience, for by the time that Artemis received her letter it was very clear that Princess Bathildis would not dream of surrendering her dignities to an English girl of inferior birth.

The ladies of Horn passed their time as Artemis had first seen them, sitting beside a porcelain stove in a draughty salon, talking about the members of princely families – their marriages, marriage prospects, children and ailments. They embroidered roses and left the backgrounds to be filled in by their ladies-in-waiting. Those ladies were always present, standing and smiling and curtseying. When the princesses retired to the ministrations of their maids, the ladies waited in an anteroom, where they might sit down to repeat and enhance the gossip they had heard from their serene Highness's lips.

It was not done for noble ladies to take exercise, though they were occasionally driven rather slowly along a road that had been swept clear of snow for that purpose. It was not done to speak of people who were not noble, or of subjects that might conceivably be controversial. It was not done to be interested in outside affairs.

'It is a duty that we owe the Prince, to express no opinions,' Artemis was told, and,

'It is a duty that we owe our rank to keep our distance from our inferiors.'

The fact that Artemis spoke French and German did nothing to endear her to her new family. A wife who could not produce a counter in the game of inheritance and alliance was of no interest. Artemis was asked nothing about her own home, and rebuked if she did not behave properly as a member of her new one.

'It is a duty that we owe ourselves, always to consider the effect that our words or deeds may have on others.'

They were always afraid that anything they did might be held against them and were sure that everybody watched them, all the time, for signs of favouritism or indiscretion. All the ladies were continuously conscious of their own positions and carried themselves with stiff backs and high shoulders, their chins raised above stretched necks, their lips smiling, their eyes blank.

'Naturally we are always observed,' Ulrike told Artemis. 'That is what we are for.'

Even when there were no guests, stiff ceremony was maintained, both in the salons where the ladies spent their days, and at meals, where the gentlemen joined them. The dining room was lined with footmen and with the ladies-in-waiting, who remained standing, to eat, presumably, later, since their figures made it evident that they ate abundantly and often. Artemis was despised for her small appetite.

'It is fortunate that she need not display the family jewels.' Princess Bathildis had not passed to her daughter-in-law any of the Horn jewels, but wore them scattered liberally on her own broad bosom.

Each place at the dinner table was provided with blue glass finger bowls inside which were matching tumblers containing a peppermint and water mixture. At the end of the meal, both ladies and gentlemen took a mouthful of the water, gargled noisily and spat out into the bowls. In order of precedence everyone then passed into one of the salons, where each member of the family then kissed all the others, saying 'Good digestion' as they did so. The ladies received Artemis's brushing cheek against theirs coldly, and Prince Waldemar pecked at the air an inch away from her chin.

My new brother does not seem to have become reconciled to my existence, dear Clementine, Artemis wrote. *I recently heard him speaking to my husband, when they were walking under my window.*

Waldemar: *Did she have to be English? Of all races the least likeable.*

Joachim: *My dear fellow, I fell in love with her.*

Waldemar: *Love – for an Englishwoman. Have you not heard Otto Bismarck's remarks on that race?*

Joachim: *If Prince Fritz himself may marry a daughter of England . . .*

Waldemar: *A scandal. But we must pray that nothing comes of it. The girl may die in childbirth. They say she's a dwarf.*

Joachim: *She's as tall as her mother who has borne a large family.*

Waldemar: *In our plans for a greater Germany, with Prussia at its helm, Bismarck says –*

Joachim: *I know what such men as Bismarck say. I've heard it on all sides. I tell you, brother, you should not believe all you hear from that man.*

Dearest sister, Artemis wrote, *do not let Mrs Lambert know that I have stooped to eavesdropping, but please ask her whether she knows what this von Bismarck says that could make Prince Waldemar wish for the death of the Princess Royal. Can it be to do with the uniting of the German states under one strong leader, of which she once spoke to us?*

The replies that Artemis received to her letters have not survived. But Clementine must have written warning her to be careful.

You are right, dear sister, to remind me that other eyes than yours and Mrs Lambert's may see my words, Artemis wrote, and she did not write of political matters again from her husband's house. Instead she described the ephemera of life in a princely household.

I came upon my sister, Princess Ulrike, in the orangery, with her daughter Augusta, who was walking from tub to tub of the sweet scented trees.

Augusta: *Good day, Madame, has it not been a fine day?*

Ulrike: *Smile, Augusta. Princesses must always smile.*

Augusta: (smiling) *Good day, Monsieur, we are pleased to see you at court. Have you been for a ride today? Good afternoon, Madame, I am enchanted to make your acquaintance. Have you a large family?*

Ulrike: *As you see, Augusta is learning to make her* cercle.

Augusta: *The trees stand for courtiers, Aunt. Good day, Your Excellency, is it not a pleasant day?*

Ulrike: *A princess must* cercler *gracefully. I was taught to do it around the trees at home in Weimar.*

Artemis: *It is a fine art, I can see.*

Ulrike: *It is one at which a princess should excel. I am admired for my skill at it. Augusta, you may listen to Mamma; once I noticed that a courtier was carrying black gloves. I said that I regretted to hear of his bereavement, and he was naturally overcome with gratitude that I had remembered. Of course I knew nothing of it. I tell you this, Augusta, to remind you how much the people value our attentions. It is not the same in your position, Artemis.*

Augusta: *What is Aunt Artemis's position, Mamma?*

Ulrike: *She is not a proper wife for a prince, my dear, she is not high and well born. In any case, she is an Englishwoman.*

V

Jeremy Ellice noticed Tamara's reaction when he brought the tea in a silver pot on a tray made of polished wood with scalloped edges and a shell design in marqueterie. The cups were transparent porcelain with a design of dragons.

'I am a perfectionist,' he explained. 'Either I have what I really admire or I do without. That's why you are sitting on a deck chair.'

'Your things are lovely,' Tamara said.

'And genuine.'

'You don't go in for replicas or reproductions?'

Jeremy made a face at the very idea. 'They wouldn't feel the same.'

'I am never sure about that. Made from the same pattern book, with similar tools, in identical designs – an Adam chimney piece say, or a Chippendale chair, would you know the difference?'

'And you an archaeologist! It's your job to know the difference, isn't it?'

'Yes, within limits. But I know it from facts, not feelings. All the distinctions in my type series are definable.'

'So you'd be as happy with a Van Meegeren as a Vermeer?' Jeremy said.

'That's a school essay subject!' Tamara protested, laughing. 'It was one of the questions in my A-level exams. I said I would be. If the forger's picture is as beautiful as the painter's why should I care who held the brush? I don't have too much sympathy for people who use art as an investment and then find they've chosen fakes. They should have bought for love not money in the first place.'

Jeremy poured out the pale tea. Tamara accepted a cup, and drew in the smoky scent. She said, 'I don't suppose it's so much of a problem with books, anyway. You aren't much troubled by forgers are you?'

'Not at my end of the market.'

'It must be fun to have a bookshop.'

'That's what people always think.'

'Isn't it?'

'It has its points. But I'm not rich.'

'But you deal with what you like best all day – books.'

'Dealing with them means parting with them. Every time I find something I'd once have given my life for I have to sell it to keep alive. I went into book dealing because I had a passion for them, that's true enough, but if the passion survives it's torture not to hang on to them, and if it doesn't you take agin it. If you go into trade, Tamara, choose something you are indifferent to. Not that you'll get rich, but at least you won't suffer.'

'Presumably if you sincerely want to get rich you don't choose this sort of work in the first place.'

'There's always the hope of finding a first folio of *Hamlet*. But how many young people know they'd like to have a rich old age? We used to despise material comfort in my youth. I wouldn't have had a three piece suite if you paid me to give it house room.'

'And now?' Tamara asked, shifting on the admittedly uncomfortable chair.

'Now I get rheumatism. I'd like to spend the winters in the sun and the summers in comfort. And have time to

31

read my wares. Book dealers never read books, you know.'

'So what will you do if you come across your first folio?'

'Take the money and run. Get some decent clothes, I'm fed up with being labelled by my appearance. Stop looking like a trendy lefty. Sell this house and get a place with proper bathrooms and central heating. Take taxis. Not have to worry. Become a paid up member of the bourgeoisie.'

'Would you really like that?'

'You little imagine how much,' he said sincerely, realising that Tamara did not believe him. Life was easy enough for someone like her; young, successful, well educated, and looking like the illustration from the lower class of romantic story come to life, with her yellow hair, blue eyes, pink cheeks and snub nose. Admittedly there was more character in her face than a conventional heroine would be permitted to show; she could cope with poverty or adversity, or even with plain boredom. Once, long ago, Jeremy Ellice had supposed himself to be a man of willpower and principle too. Now he would have sold anything, from his wares to his soul, for wealth and freedom. More than once he had called Beelzebub, but so far unanswered.

But this girl would not understand the despair that worldly failure induced in a man who had once despised worldly success. She was, simply, too pretty.

Jeremy Ellice seldom admired female beauty, even though he was unpleasantly affected by its opposite and never chose to be with such women as his sister Margot. He deeply resented the assumption, on her and the hospital staff's part, that as her only relation he was now obliged to take charge of her. It was bad enough having had Margot in and out of the house these last months, since he had allowed her to keep the papers she was working on in his attic back room. But now, having to wash and feed her, and surrender his own room to her, was beyond the limit. How intensely, he thought, I dislike nurturing and nourishing. Even taking care of oneself is a boring burden, though the price one paid for being free from other ties. But if ever he did find and sell that first folio of *Hamlet*, a well trained personal servant would be his first priority; a Chinese, perhaps, or a Malay, a quiet, soft footed, respectful young man.

Jeremy Ellice had been married at one time; the first part of his life had a conventional pattern. He had attended a public school and university. He had even spent a few years climbing up an oil company's career structure. His present way of life, while not what he would have chosen since he was not rich enough to live the ideal life, was still, in his mind, infinitely preferable to what he had formerly experienced. He thought, mocking himself, I might even be a top manager by now. Like Bill Agnew.

Margot's ex-husband conformed to his stereotype. Even abandoning Margot for a pretty young secretary had been exactly what men in his position were expected to do. Not that the girl was in for a very jolly life, if Margot's accounts of the Middle-Eastern sink she had lived in were accurate. Of course, her account of it was hardly dispassionate.

Jeremy Ellice shuddered slightly at the memory of the arrival of his bitter, resentful, man-hating elder sister on his doorstep; a wet night, a heap of luggage, a taxi driver waiting for him to pay for the long journey from Heathrow. 'I have nobody else to turn to,' Margot had said. 'You are all I have left.' She did not quite say that blood was thicker than water. Looking at this elderly stranger, Jeremy doubted that it was. He was bounced into welcoming her, though he drew the line, that time, at surrendering his own bed. Margot installed herself in the attic room, where she seemed prepared to remain. She talked a good deal, and repetitively, about their shared childhood, although Jeremy remembered little of it. She related the sad saga of her married life, during which Bill had expected to be served and waited on, and to have his ancient mother nursed by his wife. She repeated ill digested chunks of feminist dogma, derived from the magazines she had read at the country club in a nation where western ideas of liberation seemed positively frivolous, compared with the servile lives the native women led. She bemoaned her own ill fortune. 'I should have gone to a university like you, Jeremy. I should have had a chance to make something of myself.'

It was really in self defence that Jeremy had taken her life in hand. Brotherly love had nothing to do with it. 'There's no reason why you shouldn't write a book, if you want to,' he told her. 'One doesn't need a university education for that.' 'But my brain has atrophied.' 'Nonsense. Make a start on these papers I got in a sale.'

What had been a rather tiresome part of his job, travelling long distances to country sales, came as relief when Margot was waiting to chatter to him in his house. Otherwise Jeremy might have given the sale on Dartmoor a miss. But the trip had been useful in another way. Reading a local paper at breakfast because the London papers had missed the train to the south west, Jeremy had seen Mrs Hoyland's advertisement for someone to live with and look after her father.

'But I don't want to look after more geriatrics,' Margot had cried. 'I have wasted the best years of my life doing that. I hate looking after people.'

So do I, Jeremy thought. He was damned if he would look after this woman, tied to him by illusory bonds, any

34

longer. Allowing her to keep the Bessemer papers in the attic room she had taken to calling hers was his final concession, though he hoped never to hear any more about self-supporting women of the nineteenth century. Margot had decided that Artemis Bessemer was a perfect example of the type, and was working on a thesis about her. 'I know I can't get a contract from a publisher, or even be helped with the research. Not without qualifications.' He diverted her from another 'if only' monologue. 'You'll be able to make something very interesting. Someone is sure to publish it.'

Artemis Bessemer was an example of a woman who first had, and then was, a lady-in-waiting, but her story would illustrate the life of any 'lady companion' whether in a palace or a suburban villa. Margot had spent months entering on filing cards the details of the indignities such women suffered. They were used to being pampered and indulged, and, above all, obeyed. They found themselves bullied or slighted once they undertook that genteel servitude. Those who had been educated to ring bells, had to answer them. Ringing bells, Margot said, was the great divide in that society. Her plan was to show that it was only an extreme example of that pattern when a duchess or countess who lived like a queen in her own household was treated as an inferior in a royal one. Accustomed to life as the mistress of a mansion, the Queen's Lady would find herself lodged in rooms so small she might have had to write her letters sitting on the bed. Dignified grandmothers had to ask, and were often refused, permission to receive visitors or to go out of the palace bounds. Those whose habit had been to summon and dismiss their own servants, were rung for and told to leave with equal authority.

'This is all very interesting so far, as a matter of fact,' Tamara told Jeremy with some surprise. Somehow the

35

dreary looking woman who had moved in to look after Grandpapa did not seem the type to produce anything worth reading. 'It can't all be invented.'

'Certainly not. Margot is the least imaginative woman I know. It's all out of the Bessemer papers. They are in a heap in my attic.'

'Where do they come from?'

'From your part of the world. Dartmoor. It's really pure chance in my trade which of the country sales one picks on; there are far too many to go to them all. Anyway, I got some quite useful books, and this rusty tin trunk that didn't seem to have been opened for God knows how long, with the name *Lady Clementine Bessemer* painted on it. When Margot was helping me sort out the job lot, she found the letters in the trunk.'

'All this material? What luck.'

'Yes – diaries, letters, dance programmes, service sheets, invitations, all the impedimenta of an upper class young lady, quite untouched as far as one could tell. Screeds of letters from this Artemis, but all one sided. Clementine's diary petered out when she grew up. Nothing after she was about eighteen.'

'Who has Margot shown it to?' Tamara asked.

'Nobody, as far as I know. She doesn't know too many people in London.'

'Surely . . . some contemporary Bessemers . . . ?'

'None in *Who's Who* or *Whitaker's Almanac*. Margot has written to the present Prince of Horn, but I don't think she's had a reply yet.'

'One of Artemis's descendants?'

'I don't know. I haven't read everything yet. Why don't you have another cup and carry on with the typescript while I just nip downstairs to see if Margot wants anything.?'

VI

For Christmas, the Family moved to another of its castles, Drachenschloss. Although this residence had fewer rooms than Horn, where there was said to be one for each day of the year, it was an immense edifice made of red stone erected over a reddish mountain, in whose living rock some of the rooms actually were.

The peak was visible from far away, but Artemis thought at first that what she saw looming ahead was a natural feature of the landscape, not realising that its tip consisted of the castle. It dominated the surrounding district of forests and lower hills. A deep gorge separated the rock from the surrounding landscape, and a bridge over this rocky chasm was the only approach to the castle.

'It has never fallen in any siege,' Prince Joachim told his wife. 'My family has reigned here for a thousand years.'

All the gothic tales she had ever read flickered through Artemis's memory. Surely here, if anywhere, she would encounter the horrors that had evoked such delicious shivers when they were only the stuff of fiction? But adventure and her new relations could hardly be mentioned in the same sentence, so prosaic in behaviour and appearance were they. These stout ladies would not appeal to the least fastidious vampire and Joachim was different indeed from the saturnine villains of story. Artemis pulled her new furs about her and gazed steadily at what was, she told herself, no more than an inconvenient house. 'How,' she asked, 'is the castle heated? It must be very damp.'

Artemis wrote to Clementine and Mrs Lambert that afternoon:

You would think it most beautiful, with ranges of snow clad hills visible from my windows, and everywhere the sound of the waterfall that drops over the mountainside. My apartments are in better repair than those I occupy at Horn, and the tapestries hanging over the stone walls keep at bay at least some of the damp, cold air. No ceremony is relaxed here. My lady still attends me all the time and in my dressing room I am always assisted by three maids. Footmen wait day and night outside my door, to escort me wherever I go, even into a neighbouring room, and no member of the family enters the apartments of another unannounced. However many times a day we meet, we shake hands with one another, over and over again. Outriders follow my carriage when I drive, servants walk behind me even in the pleasure grounds. None of these rules are changed here, I find, though I had expected that things might be different in this fortress. Well do I remember the liberty we enjoyed at home.

The wife of the reigning prince might have expected to be free. Artemis nearly died in one attempt at independence.

She had managed to give her warders the slip – she was, after all, as young as a modern schoolgirl, and she enjoyed mischief even without an accomplice. She wrote to Clementine:

I had noted that one of the chambers in the long passage leading to my own apartments was not in use. One of my husband's great aunts had died there as a young girl, disappointed in love, I have been told. By allowing my ladies to suppose that I was with my maids, my maids to think that the footman was with me, and by telling the footman to announce me to this empty room in which I said I was to meet his highness, I found myself alone. I can hardly express to you, dear, distant sister, what that sensation was like after all these months. To be unattended in a room, without every move observed and criticised, relieved of the anxiety lest I do something that could be disapprovingly described to my husband or to my new mamma, was as liberty must feel to a captive newly released from gaol. For a while I simply sat and took my pleasure in solitude. The room was very cold, for I think that it had been unused for fifty years at least. The story I have heard only in whispers from my maids, but I believe it to be that the wretched occupant of the room took her own life when her lover was killed in the wars. I suppose that he was an officer in the army of Bonaparte, for there is still a miniature portrait on a table in the room framed in crumbling laurel leaves.

The relics of that distant love brought philosophical speculations into Artemis's mind of which she wrote at length to Clementine. One can imagine her, like Hamlet with Yorick's skull, soliloquising about mortality. She even quoted him: '*If this had not been a gentlewoman, she should have been buried out of Christian burial.*'

I do not believe, Artemis wrote, *that crowner's quest law, as the gravedigger has it, applies to my new family any more than other laws. They are all-powerful here. And had I perished that day, would any coroner have sat on me?*

After a while, Artemis had begun to explore the room. She found the dead girl's toilet articles both repulsive and pathetic. *If this were indeed my house to command, this whole mausoleum should be emptied and refurbished. I deplore this morbid superstition.*

The room was in the corner of the main tower of the castle, and doors on either side of the bed led into closets. The first contained what Artemis described as '*a necessary article*'. The other was the dressing room. Obsolete garments lay on the shelves where they had been put fifty years before. A slit window gave a little daylight, and Artemis was peering through it at the fearsome drop below when she heard the door behind her close.

Yet there was no draught, for I had not opened the window; and then I heard another door close more softly, as though somebody had gone out of the bedroom. But, Clementine, when I turned the handle of the closet door, it would not budge. I was imprisoned! Solitude indeed I had desired, but not solitary confinement. For confined I found myself to be. I called, but I knew as I did so that my voice could never be heard, for the closet had walls party to no other room, being those of a semicircular turret, and I was separated from the passage along which the family and servants might pass by two thick, closed doors. You may imagine my thoughts, dear sister. Was it an accident that had locked the door of the closet? Was it possible that the hand of an unknown enemy had turned the key? Would I die here, in cold and hunger? Indeed, I began to believe so, to believe it to be no joke, for my hands were bleeding and my voice hoarse, and still I was unheard and the door of my cage unmoved. Would my starved corpse be discovered, wrapped in the ancient cloak of that other girl who went untimely to her death? Much did I think in that time of my short life, and, dear sister, of my love for you, and the grief that the news of my demise must bring you. I thought too of eternity, and of those mysteries that we have so often pondered together. I thought but little of my new family. None, I believe, would truly regret me, and sitting in that darkening prison, I wondered whether it was one of them who had watched me entering the empty room, and taken the opportunity to rid the family of its English interloper. But I shall say no more of that. You will readily imagine what awful thoughts come to the mind when death seems imminent.

It must have been three, even four hours, before I was saved. I had fallen into an uneasy doze. The voices I heard seemed insubstantial at first, as though part of my dream, or conjured into being by the urgency of my desire. Soon, however, I did realise that two human beings of solid flesh and blood had crept into the bedroom outside my door. I understand but little of the dialect spoken by the peasants, but I heard enough to understand that this was not the first time this room had been used for their rendezvous by a footman and a chambermaid, and that the man said he had been keeping watch on the passage outside, and had seen nobody pass since His Highness hours before. At this point he heard my feeble tapping at the closet door which he flung open in terror, supposing me to be a ghost I truly believe, for his face was blanched, the lips grinning in fear and the eyes glazed. The girl had buried her face in the pillow. I was almost fainting, but the man made no move to help me even after he recognised me, muttering those familiar words, 'The Englishwoman'. Had I the presence of mind the wife of a reigning prince should command, I would have made much of their improper and disrespectful behaviour. As it was I tottered past, under their hostile gaze, and returned to my own apartments. As a consequence of this adventure, I have been confined to my couch for two days, affected by cold and fear, and by a disorder of the digestion.

Artemis drew no parallel between her own unpleasant experience and those that regularly befell the heroines of those gothic novels that had come into her mind at the first sight of Drachenschloss. Yet a dispassionate reader must wonder whether it was mere chance or mischief that had led Artemis so close to death. If it had not been for two servants finding

40

themselves a private bed (instead of the crowded hovels they were used to) Artemis might well have died in that closet. She may herself have had more precise suspicions than she cared or dared to put in writing. She was always circumspect, although she made no attempt to pretend to a happiness that she could not feel, but the problems on which she most needed advice could not be put into writing by a girl of her time and her references to them are periphrastic in the extreme, though it was clearly about this time that she realised she was pregnant. She wrote more about the way her days were spent, a depressing chronicle of petty samenesses. Monotonous embroidery and gossip about the same small group of eligible people were unending. The doings of those below noble rank were of no interest to the ladies, and the peasants who worked the land and the mines were not regarded as human beings at all. When the ladies went out driving they ignored the servile salutes of the local inhabitants, and the outriders would whip children out of the coach's way with the same indifference that they felt for stray dogs. When Artemis enquired about the kind of charitable and educational work that most English ladies thought their duty on their country estates, and that Mrs Lambert had tried to do in Lady Bessemer's place, her suggestion was greeted with disgusted incomprehension. *The ladies tell me that it is not princely to think of such things. They find my ideas distasteful. It is not for the nobility to sully itself with the workers' concerns.*

Drachenschloss was an extremely uncomfortable house to live in. The princely family ate cold food, washed in cold water, and shivered beside inadequate fires in the damp depths of the castle. Artemis's request for a bath was ignored, and she was permitted to change nothing in her rooms, but once she was resigned to the permanent company of lackeys and ladies she began to explore this ancient seat of the family of Horn. She realised that it was the centre of immense industry. Her husband was said to give employment to more than seven thousand men on these estates, working the farms and the mines, and there were innumerable servants, most of whom seemed to live far within the rock itself in conditions of which Artemis shuddered to think. The most privileged employees were the huntsmen; there were hundreds, making up a semi-military corps. The internal arrangements of the castle had not been altered for centuries, but Joachim talked of modernising and building on. One detail, however, would never be permitted to change, and that Artemis was shown on Christmas Day.

A formal visitation was made by the Family, who walked down through passages and stairways they normally avoided, to a dungeon, barred from casual intruders by a huge, mediaeval oak door, studded with iron nails, and unlocked by a key nearly a foot long.

Down here, within the rock, water dripped eternally down the walls and daylight could never penetrate. Artemis felt as though she had been transported into another era, away from the rococo salons, the dining room with its renaissance decoration, the mediaeval chambers last modernised in the fifteenth century. Here was the heart of Drachenschloss, Artemis thought, and shook herself to dispel superstition to which she had been as much prey, for a moment, as all the Family.

The Chief Master of Ceremonies offered the key to the Prince on a golden salver. The Prince inserted it into the blackened whorls of lock. Within, candles had already been lighted in the wall sconces and there was less dust on the treasure chest than on the furniture in Artemis's own room.

The chest consisted of an elaborately wrought coffer made of panels of rock crystal, with a dome shaped lid through which the treasure could be seen. Artemis had not known what to expect. Her ideas had ranged from a heap of gold coins to a carved statue.

Imagine my horror, dear sister, to see before me the preserved face of a man long since dead. Preserved, I say, but horribly altered, darkened and shrunk in upon itself, the teeth protruding, the skin wrinkled – but I shall write no more on so abhorrent a matter, but to mention that the awful head, and I suppose the body too, was encased in rusty armour; the hands were clasped on the chest, holding a bejewelled golden cup! That is the treasure, that, and a sword, broken and rusted like the armour, but with uncut stones set into its handle, and, the most macabre of all this dreadful sight, a coronet or crown encircling the helmet, made of dull, darkened metal through which no fugitive gleam of silver shone, and set with precious stones. The crown is said to contain a fragment of our Lord's True Cross, and all the family signed themselves and bowed to this idolatrous relic although it is not the custom in their church, but, 'it is the custom in our family', my Mamma informed me, and I was forced to follow suit, though I need not tell you how reluctantly, for blind worship is not in my nature, after the free-thinking childhood and education that you and I, dear Clementine, enjoyed. The final item in the treasure was at the finger of one of those gauntlet gloves, covering heaven knows what horror, and I could scarcely bear to rest my eyes upon it – a huge purple stone on which a face is carved, bisected with a faint line like the mark of Cain. These eternal stones, precious in our terminology, and the transient flesh of their guardian, have turned my thoughts, dear sister . . . Here the narrative of Artemis's letter is interrupted by a page of philosophical reflection on the brevity of human life and aspiration, but later she quotes the brief explanation she was given.

Joachim: *Here lies a knight of the Teutonic Order.*

Artemis: *Unburied, I see.*

Joachim: *He is our ancestor, the founder of our House.*

Artemis: *And his treasure?*

Joachim: *It belonged to Charles the Great. It is now the symbol of our House of Horn. While it endures, we endure. It came with us, and we shall go with it.*

VII

'The Horn Treasure!' Tamara exclaimed.

Jeremy Ellice had come upstairs again, carrying a shopping basket. 'Have you heard of it before?'

'I should have recognised the name at once. It's one of the famous European treasures. Had you heard of it before?'

'I have read Margot's draft. And it's mentioned in the paper. It's in the list of pieces the East Germans might send over for that exhibition.'

'Oh yes, you read that when we were downstairs. Did they say it was coming here?'

'They seemed to think . . .'

'Or was it just one of the things the East Germans are known to have stashed away somewhere? It's fabulous. Literally.'

A treasure all the more fabulous, in the modern sense of the word, for being only fabled. No modern scholar had been allowed to see it, and its continued existence was known only in rumour.

'I should have recognised the name at once,' Tamara said.

'What is it? You obviously know.'

'It's part of the regalia of Charlemagne. Or the Carolingian kings, at any rate.'

'What's it doing in Eastern Europe?'

'Treasures got scattered throughout the centuries. Years

44

of anarchy when it was finders keepers and devil take the hindmost. Bandits grabbing things and keeping or hiding them. I expect the Teutonic knight who was the ancestor of the respectable Horn family came by his wealth in ways his heirs wouldn't have been proud of.'

'It's a real treasure, is it?' Jeremy asked, passing his tongue over his dry lips.

'If it's what I think, yes. Priceless – and unique too. It's awful to think of the things there must have been and how little has survived. Lost, melted down, buried, hidden – tragic.'

'But this one, the Horn Treasure, as you called it. What did it consist of?'

'I should have to look it up. I can go to the library tomorrow.'

'You don't think there might be something here, upstairs?'

They looked, but the rows of archaeological books did not include the old volume published in Paris that Tamara believed to contain a drawing of the Horn Treasure.

'Take Margot's stuff with you, then,' Jeremy said. 'You can – I mean, I'm sure she would be grateful if you looked it up for her.' He picked up the blue folder and handed it to Tamara, still holding on to the basket in the other hand.

Tamara said, 'Are you going out?'

'It's difficult. There are some things I need, but . . .'

'I can stay if you like. I'll listen for Margot.'

'It wouldn't matter, you see, usually, but with Margot landing herself here . . .'

'That's all right. Really. It's all right.'

'I don't suppose anyone will come. People usually telephone . . .'

'Honestly, Jeremy, do go on out. I'm sure I can cope.'

He left after considerably more dithering, promising to be back very soon.

Tamara listened to the noises of the building. The windows rattled. Expanding or contracting floor boards made irregular cracks or pops. No sound from downstairs, where Margot was still asleep. Sitting on the canvas chair beside the hissing gas fire, Tamara's eyes closed.

The bell woke her to disorientation. It took her a moment to realise where she was and that she must have heard Margot Ellice's summons. She stumbled on the dark stairs, and fumbled for the light switch, first in the downstairs lobby, and then in the big room. But Margot Ellice was still asleep, her drawn, bony face withdrawn from awareness. Tamara started up the stairs again.

The front door was open. He was standing at the top of the stairs, a man about six feet tall, immense up there above her in the gloom.

Tamara ran up, so that he stepped back. A long, straight boned face, short hair, the eyes and mouth of a handsome man; he wore a good flannel suit, and a polo necked jersey.

'Was it you who rang?'

'Yes, but when I found the door was not closed, I came in. I suppose the shop is open? It's only . . .' He shook his watch forward to see the time. He had strapped it over a bandage that covered his palm and wrist. 'It looks ridiculous, doesn't it? I had a slight disagreement with a cat. But your health service is marvellous.' He spoke the excessively faultless English of a bilingual foreigner; Dutch or Scandinavian, perhaps.

Tamara had almost forgotten she was in a shop. She said hastily, 'Of course. Can I help you?'

'May I just have a look round?'

'Yes, do. I mean, I'm sure that's all right. I'm just minding the shop for the owner.'

'Ah. I thought you didn't look quite what I expected.'

His eyes were that very piercing blue that Tamara unscientifically associated with sexiness, under feather

46

shaped, slightly glossy eyebrows: mid-thirties, probably, or perhaps older, forty even. A beautiful man, she thought appreciatively, remembering how her dead lover, Ian Barnes, always insisted that men could be handsome but not beautiful. But then he had been neither himself.

The man moved around the room, taking books from the shelves, leafing through them and replacing them.

'Are you looking for anything in particular?' Tamara said.

'I am interested in art history. I deal in fine art.'

'Really? Do you specialise at all?'

'Paintings, sculpture, objets d'art.'

'Well, I think upstairs is the place to look.' Tamara heard Margot call her name from below. 'Can you manage? I must just go down a moment – there's an invalid in the house.'

'Of course. Don't bother about me.'

Margot wanted a drink and an audience. She was peevish at Jeremy's absence. 'You would have thought – I mean, it's not as though . . .' She thought it was his duty to stay by her side.

Tamara plumped the sour smelling pillows and left the full glass within easy reach. 'I must go upstairs, Margot, there's a customer.'

'Really, it's too bad. Jeremy shouldn't . . .'

'Not a bit. I'm enjoying myself.'

Up again to the beautiful young man.

Surprised at herself, Tamara thought the words, I really fancy him.

He was standing by the fireplace, reading the typescript of Margot's work.

'I'm so sorry,' Tamara took it from his hands, and adjusted the rubber bands over the blue cardboard folder. 'That isn't part of the stock. It's something I'm reading for a friend.'

47

'It looks interesting,' he said. 'Are you a historian?'

'I am an archaeologist.'

'We are allies, then. Though most prehistory is beyond me.'

'What period do you specialise in?'

'I don't specialise. I supply what clients tell me they want. At present I'm in London on behalf of an American client.'

'You mean, they tell you to find them a Rembrandt?'

'It is not so difficult as you make it sound. Tomorrow I shall look at an alleged Giotto. I have a good eye.'

Tamara stared into his good eyes. If our genders were reversed, she thought, I'd pinch his bottom. And then I'd ask him if he was doing anything tonight. And then . . . but it was the wrong place and time. The shadowed books, climbing out of sight in the dusk, muffled their words. The thought flashed through Tamara's mind that she was in a graveyard, where high ambitions were buried. What greater intimation of futility could there be than the sight of these forgotten offerings?

'A Giotto?' she said. 'It doesn't sound likely.'

He turned at the sound of the front door slamming closed. Jeremy Ellice came into the room, carrying his loaded basket, his sparse, dark hair stuck by rain to his forehead.

'A customer, Jeremy,' Tamara said.

'I came in to have a look at your art books,' the customer said.

Jeremy turned on the lights to show the way upstairs. 'Was there anything in particular?'

Margot's voice came faintly up. 'Is that you, Jem? Have you got my tablets?' Jeremy's lips tautened and he darted an unloving look in the direction of his sister's summons.

'You'll have to excuse me for a moment. Would you go on up? Tamara, I'm eternally grateful, goodbye.' Her coat was on the banisters, and he held it out for her, before going down the stairs.

Tamara opened the front door, and found that the customer was following her down the steps. She said, 'What about your books?'

'I shall look in a moment. Tamara. A pretty name.'

'Tamara Hoyland.'

'Kim Rice.'

'How do you do.'

'Just at present I do extremely well, thank you, and if you come to lunch with me tomorrow and look at the Giotto with me, I shall do even better.'

'Alleged Giotto.'

'The Tate Gallery? One o'clock?'

I made him say that, she thought, pulling away from the kerb in her tiny yellow car. I willed it.

Tamara turned the car in a neighbour's drive. Kim Rice was still watching her, standing beside the open front door that seemed so unlikely an entrance to an emporium of books. Were many ordinary looking houses in residential streets places where commercial treasures changed hands? It threw a new light on suburban London.

But then, she reminded herself, anything can happen behind our secretive front doors. Only a few miles downhill and to the south was the house in Bayswater where Tamara had learnt the skills that had put Margot's attacker to flight. It was called, on a tiny sign fixed to its railings, *Health and Happiness House for Ladies and Gentlemen*. I got more than a tanned skin and flat tummy there, she thought, weaving through the traffic with a verve that a different instructor had refined; and when she opened the front door of the house she lived in, her lips twitched in amusement at her own automatic caution as she obeyed the well-remembered rules: to fling the door inwards standing to one side; to listen before entering; to climb the stairs inaudibly; to act, if she

49

was going to act, without hesitation. Yes, the faces of houses and of people could be equally well disguised.

Tamara Hoyland had completely redecorated her apartment since Ian Barnes, who had lived in it with her, died. Its contents had been sparse and mechanical, and she had replaced them with the kind of things that might have furnished this early nineteenth-century house when it was first built. She had painted the walls a sunny yellow, introduced an Empire bed, an embroidered carpet and chintz curtains. Winter flowering jasmine was creeping all over the large skylight and on the window sills pots of hyacinths and daffodils were just coming into bloom. The impression was of an old fashioned room in the country, but the gadgets were modern

Electronic eyes tracked the faces of callers to the house, and of those who were admitted to climb the stairs and wait outside Tamara's fortified door. A system of bells and lights would frighten any intruder who managed, improbably, to breach the outer defences; another system carried immediate warnings to permanently manned guardrooms whence rescuers coud be instantly dispatched. Disguised switches could activate recorders of sight and sound. Booby traps awaited unwary attackers, not least the booby trap that a ferociously trained and experienced Tamara represented to anyone who supposed her to be a weak or submissive female.

After two years of working for Department E, Tamara was accustomed to the precautions she took and the protection she attracted, and had never, in fact, needed to activate it. To her, the fortified room was a homely refuge and her daily life in it was unsophisticated, and hardly aided by modern gadgetry, so now she filled a rubber hot water bottle from a kettle boiled on a gas ring, and went to bed, with Margot's manuscript, in bedsocks.

50

VIII

Artemis von Horn grew rapidly resigned to the unpopularity of her own country in Prussia. Later evidence confirms the impression she recorded in her letters; for instance, an observer recorded that the Queen of Prussia's Mistress of the Robes refused to be introduced to a British diplomat, and a Prussian officer's wife leant across her neighbour, an English lady, at a state banquet, to complain to the Prussian on her other side, '*Je déteste les Anglaises.*'

The Princess Royal of England, Princess Frederick William of Prussia, caused offence from the very beginning of her married life by having the ceremony in England. Everyone in Germany inferred that she had the wrong attitude towards her new country, and Artemis heard much gossip to that effect, in the weeks after her own, and before the royal marriage.

In the middle of January, Joachim and Artemis were summoned to Berlin to greet the royal couple on their arrival. Artemis was relieved to be without her gaggle of new relations, since none of them chose to welcome the English alliance. Joachim was a friend of Prince Frederick William. They had studied together at the University of Bonn, where they had discussed reforms and liberalisation, and an additional message had commanded Artemis's presence. 'Her Royal Highness will be pleased to see the face of another English bride.'

Every man wore uniform, every woman many-layered skirts, with bare shoulders. The Court waited at the top of the Grand Staircase in the palace until cheering, unusual in Berlin, showed that the party had arrived. Artemis told

51

Clementine how the Princess Royal had come running up the steps to sink in a low curtsey before her father-in-law, the Prince of Prussia, whom she had known in London. *His Royal Highness had moved aside to greet his son before the Princess rose, her cheek tilted for the kiss he did not bestow, and I heard the Queen say, 'You must be very cold.' They say that the Queen is another who regrets the English match. But Her Royal Highness was quickly tactful. 'I have only one warm place, and that is my heart.' To me, as she made her cercle, she said, 'I shall be glad to number you among my ladies.' Little did we imagine, dear Clementine, that the day would come when one of us was to be an attendant upon a future Queen of Prussia! Yet I believe it may be an agreeable experience for me. HRH has not the air of one who is unhappy, or who has been forced into an unwelcome match for reasons of state.*

Artemis must have looked for traces of similar coercion to that she had experienced, but the Princess Royal, unlike her, was blissfully happy, and Artemis did find that she enjoyed being at court. She found herself in the company of friendly girls of her own age, for the highborn dowagers appointed to the English Princess's entourage only appeared on formal occasions and the Countess Perponcher, who was nominally in charge of the younger ladies-in-waiting, was pregnant and unwell. Vicky spent most of her time with the two young Prussian girls, Walpurga von Hohenthal and Marie Lynar, and with Artemis. They played schoolroom games together, ludo or draughts or halma, and, when they felt energetic, chased each other along the marble corridors of the Berliner Schloss, playing hide-and-seek in the dark, stuffy rooms, or frightening each other with macabre stories about the local ghost, known as the White Lady. They sang part-songs, painted, modelled in clay, and even carried on their education. Princess Vicky was glad to discuss the politics and history she had studied, and used to write essays on such topics as Ministerial Responsibility which she sent home for her father to correct.

Prussian men spent their time on military manoeuvres, from dawn until dusk and after.

The Princess Royal: *Isn't it hard on wives like ourselves, Artemis, that our husbands are always busy elsewhere.*

Artemis: *It seems to be the lot of Prussian ladies, Ma'am.*

HRH (almost in tears): *At home Papa and Mamma are always together. This is not what I expected at all.*

I wonder what she did expect, Artemis wrote to Clementine. At the same time Vicky was writing to the Queen that her ladies were more like sisters than servants to her. Artemis's letters do not give the impression that she felt sisterly emotions towards her royal mistress. The gulf fixed by royalty between itself and its servants was too wide for Vicky to know what real friendship between girls of eighteen could be. She said that her ladies were respectful, and so they had to be. The Queen had warned her daughter, 'No familiarity, no loud laughing; kindness, friendliness and civility, but no familiarity except with your parents-in-law. Never let yourself go, or forget what you owe to yourself.'

Wally Hohenthal and Marie Lynar accepted Vicky's occasionally chilling dignity without question, but Artemis had not been educated to revere the institution of royalty; rather, Mrs Lambert had spoken wistfully of the times she recalled from her own youth when all the thrones of Europe were tottering. Even Queen Victoria wondered then whether she should train her children for life as commoners. Mrs Lambert could remember the present, now senile, King of Prussia, when he had been forced to appease the populace by riding round Berlin saluting the bodies of the demonstrators his soldiers had shot, and handing out democratic pamphlets. At the same time his brother (now Vicky's father-in-law) had fled to exile in London. It would probably be high treason to mention those days in the Berlin of 1858, but Artemis often thought about them when she watched the stately processions of the Hohenzollerns at their court. The English Princess Royal was probably the only one of them who felt anything but a bored distaste for the ordinary people they ruled.

HRH: *At home it is a lady's duty to tend her poor.*

The Princess of Prussia (her mother-in-law): *Here a lady's duty is to tend her prayers and her family.*

HRH: *At home we have encouraged the provision of museums and art galleries for the people, of public libraries and charitable hospitals.*

The Mistress of the Robes: *The English Princess does not think that Prussia is good enough for her.*

HRH: *It is for us to initiate improvements.*

The Princess of Prussia: *It is not for you to decide where they are needed.*

HRH (weeping): *Papa has always taught me to say what I know to be right. Speak the truth and shame the devil.*

In the same way that the princely family of Horn had ignored their attendants, who stood waiting to serve them in silence, the Prussian Royal Family ignored Artemis or Wally or Marie as they waited, not daring to lean against the wall; Artemis tried to distract her mind from her own physical malaises (she was feeling sick, and her back ached) by remembering details to write in her letters to Clementine. She saw that the English connection was increasingly unpopular. The Princess Royal's education had reinforced her natural stubbornness, and in any case, no princess brought up in the artificial environment of a court could be expected to recognise her own limitations. Vicky's pretty manners concealed an ineradicable arrogance and self-will.

One of the things Vicky was determined to do was explore the town of Berlin; this had not been forbidden, only because it never crossed anyone's mind that she could think of such a thing.

HRH: *We shall go incognita.*

Marie: *Oh, Ma'am, I don't think we should. Your RH will be recognised.*

HRH: *There is no reason why we should seem different from other ladies.*

Wally: *But, Ma'am, other ladies do not do such things in Berlin.*

Marie: *But, Ma'am, your coachman's livery will be known at once.*

HRH: *Nonsense, I have made up my mind. Tell the coachman to stop. I intend to walk.*

(HRH walks, followed by ladies who wring their hands and wail.)

HRH: *Look at the state those buildings are in. Something must be done.*

Wally: *It is only where the very poorest people live, Ma'am.*

54

HRH: *We have nothing so disgraceful at home. But it is my duty to see living conditions at their worst. Where should I look?*

Wally & Marie (chorus): *I don't know, Ma'am.*

HRH: *I am determined to find out.*

Marie (beginning to weep: she will be scolded by the Countess Perponcher for permitting this excursion): *Oh, Ma'am, please take care.*

The streets of Berlin were filthy channels between the buildings, with no paving for vehicles, no duckboards for pedestrians, or drainage of any kind. After rain, or in melting snow, they were deep in noisome mud. On main roads planks raised on stones allowed cleaner passage, but when an officer approached civilians stepped off into the mud to let him pass, and all pedestrians flattened themselves against the walls to keep clear of the unswerving troops of cavalry. No Prussian soldier would alter his course for a working class man, woman or child, nor be reprimanded if he ran one down.

HRH: *At home the military may not frighten citizens so.*

Wally: *Oh, Ma'am, you are spattered with mud. Your dress . . .*

HRH: *You observe that the only building in good repair is the barracks.*

Marie: *Oh, Ma'am, may we not return? The district is not fit for you.*

HRH: *We shall continue.*

The three ladies followed the Princess's small, determined figure into a slightly less insalubrious street in which the ground floor rooms of most houses were used as shops. Some sold books or artists' materials. A portrait was displayed in one, and when Vicky paused to look at it, she exclaimed, 'It is my Grandmamma, Papa's mamma, Princess Louise of Saxe Coburg.'

Prince Albert's mother had run away from her disreputable husband, leaving behind the two small sons whom she never saw again, and died seven years later in exile. Inventive gossips said that she had loved her Jewish Chamberlain, and that he, not the Duke, was the father of Prince Albert.

Ignoring the protests of Marie and Wally, Vicky led the way into the shop, which consisted of a tiny, dark room, with stairs

55

leading out of one corner into what must be the living quarters. The goods for sale were not displayed, but stored in leather trunks, and the counter was a small table covered with a red cloth. The shopkeeper came into the room through another door in the back wall, a bearded, patriarchal figure, with a small skull cap on his head.

Wally Hohenthal drew in her breath, and muttered, 'A Jew.'

Vicky assumed her rare, quelling dignity, and commanded her to wait outside with Marie Lynar. Artemis alone was to remain.

Artemis noted that the Princess showed no prejudice against Jews or any other class of person, perhaps because her conviction that royalty was invariably superior made all other mortals equal in her sight.

The Shopkeeper: *May I assist the noble ladies?*

HRH: *We should like to see the engraving in the window.*

Shopkeeper: *It is by Kriehuber, as the noble lady will see. The subject is not known.*

HRH: *Where does it come from?*

Shopkeeper: *I am offering it for sale on behalf of one of my humble family, noble lady. He was left it by his much mourned father, who told his family that the likeness was of a great lady he was not at liberty to name.*

When Vicky said she would buy it, the old man called for his son to carry the parcel to the main road where the coach waited. 'My son is visiting me in Berlin at present. He is a philosopher, from the University of Bonn.'

The young man who came in answer to the call of 'Philip' was not wearing the skull cap, and elsewhere would have been indistinguishable from any intellectual German. It was only in this house that one remarked the curved nose and dark hair that revealed the Jew. Artemis recognised him at once. She had seen him before, when she and Clementine spied on their governess walking with her brother.

He evidently recognised the Princess Royal, though only his first glance and deep bow showed it. He followed the ladies, carrying the package, towards the small crowd that had

56

collected around her carriage.

Artemis was overcome by emotion. *He is the first person I have seen since I left England who has any connection with my dear home. I was able to speak with him briefly. He is Philip Ehrenstamm, the brother of our dear Mrs Lambert. I wonder whether I shall be able to see him again.*

The coachman was trying to whip the people away from his gleaming coachwork and the outriders were pushing others back to clear a path for the ladies to approach. 'It is the Englishwoman,' the people were saying, with greedy stares at the Princess's silks and furs. Vicky smiled and bowed. 'English, English,' small children called, and one or two of their mothers spat on the ground.

I asked Mr Ehrenstamm whether I might call on his father, but he had time to tell me (and, dear Clementine, you will not allow Mrs Lambert to read this section of my letter) that she is dead to her family, having married out of their faith. I believe that those of the Hebrew persuasion mourn their children for the space of a week, as though they have indeed perished, when they do not marry one of their own.

None of those watching cheered as the Royal carriage drew away. Jeanette Lambert's brother bowed very low.

HRH: *When Mamma drives out in London, the people run after her with flowers.*

Wally: *Is your RH not pleased with our Prussians, then?*

HRH: *What can you mean, Wally? They are my Prussians now. This is my country.*

Marie (always the peacemaker): *They will certainly take your RH to their hearts.*

HRH: *That was the first gentleman I have seen in Prussia who did not wear uniform.*

Wally: *A Jew!*

HRH (coldly): *A philosopher.*

Marie: *I never saw my father in anything but uniform, Ma'am. No Prussian nobleman would wear anything else.*

HRH: *We shall not mention this morning's expedition, ladies.*

But they knew they could not help being found out. Very soon the Countess Perponcher would know where the Royal coach had been and add this titbit to the catalogue of Vicky's iniquities. The Royal ladies were all much offended by her dissatisfaction with their own enclosed world. In her role of invisible lady-in-waiting, Artemis heard several conversations in which it was made plain that the English Princess was expected to confine her curiosity to more suitable subjects, that is, other royalties, and their clothes and children. Male members of the family were required to think only of military matters.

The Prince of Prussia (Vicky's father-in-law): *I am interested in nothing, except being a soldier and the work of a soldier.*

HRH: *At home, princes – that is to say, my papa, is interested in everything that pertains to his country's advancement and his people's good.*

The Princess of Prussia: *I hear that the Prince Consort actually goes among the people.*

HRH: *Papa believes that he has much to learn from them.*

The Princess of Prussia: *We have nothing to learn from our inferiors.*

At a ball, while Vicky danced and Artemis stood suffering the discomforts of early pregnancy, she listened to another conversation.

The Princess of Prussia: *We have heard that she has actually been seen walking in the streets!*

Princess Charles of Prussia (an aunt): *I have heard that she has been criticising the conditions of the poor.*

The Princess of Prussia: *She speaks of such things as elections and parliament with her guests.*

Princess Charles: *I believe that she compares Berlin unfavourably with London, a city from whose dirt and disorder I was glad to escape alive.*

The Princess of Prussia: *I have even been told that she discussed the political future of Prussia with Professors from the University.*

Both Princesses (in chorus): *It must cease!*

All these accusations were true. Vicky liked to see herself as both symbol, and spur, of a newly liberal Prussia. She boasted of the words with which a liberal newspaper had greeted her arrival: 'Morality, conscience, even patriotism, have slept, but the sun is setting on the old régime, and in our new Princess we see the bright hope of the new one.'

'My court shall be like Mamma's, an example to the nation,' Vicky vowed, and made no secret of her plan to be, with her Fritz, the joint inspiration of a newly enlightened, newly united Germany. After all, the King was senile, his direct heir, Fritz's father, only three years younger, and soon Fritz and Vicky could be King and Queen of a reformed, reforming Prussia, the hope for a new Germany ruled by an English-style constitutional government.

It was this very event that such Prussians as Joachim's brother Waldemar most dreaded. The only constitutional changes they wished to see were the abolition of all concessions granted under duress in 1848. Their hope was a return to old-style autocracy, and the united Germany to which they also looked forward would be an Empire, not a free confederation. The monarchy of a weak Prince Frederick William, over-influenced by his English wife through whose voice the Prince Consort would command, was to them an appalling prospect. Better by far that the old King should live on, totally conservative in everything – 'What was good enough for my glorious ancestors is good enough for me.' He would not even permit baths to be installed in the royal palaces.

Artemis tried once to warn Vicky of the effect of her careless talk. 'There are those who do not admire liberalism or democracy as your Royal Highness does. Perhaps a little discretion . . .'

But Artemis could only marvel at the Princess's lack of that quality. What would have been amusing in a debutante or a university student was dangerous in a future queen, and Artemis found herself quoting the advice she had received herself: 'It is a duty that we owe the Prince, to express no opinions.' But Vicky would express all her opinions.

I have found, dear Clementine, that it is the habit of courtiers to speak much of the kindness of royalty, to be gratified whenever a smile is awarded them, to be moved by any sign of interest in their own affairs. Royal persons do not seem to be judged by the same standards as others; were they to be so, I doubt that the Princess Royal would be admired in spite of her intelligence and quick wits. She lacks the judgement to see,

59

among other things, that the views of a female of eighteen, no matter how well founded, can hardly influence those with more experience of the world and its affairs. Indeed, I do admire HRH's liberalism and high ideals, which I believe are shared by my husband and by hers, and in which you and I were educated too, but we no longer live in an age when the wishes of royal personages are to influence others. I fear that HRH expects to be a ruler. One cannot wonder at it, that her future subjects are not willing to be ruled by her, except in name. As for me, I find her agreeable, for her manners are perfect, but always notice that she is certain of her own superiority to all other mortals. All her friendliness cannot disguise that.

While she was at court, Artemis was able to write freely, for her letters were sent with Vicky's own by the private messenger. But two months before her baby was due Artemis left the Princess Royal, and she was almost relieved, even though it meant that she must return to the unwelcoming company of Joachim's family.

Joachim insisted that his son must be born at Drachenschloss. Ulrike said that she could not understand why he cared. 'Your son, after all, Artemis, can never inherit.' But Joachim insisted that the archaic rules of inheritance would have been reformed by the time they became relevant to his son. Prince Fritz had agreed that they should be abolished.

Artemis's child was a boy, but Joachim did not live to see him as his heir. The christening took place, as was customary, before the child was a week old. The baby was called Heinrich, followed by a string of family names, none of which was chosen by Artemis, who referred to him as 'Baby'. Before Artemis was allowed to leave her couch (since certain death was promised to women who put their feet to the ground within three weeks of childbirth, unless the women were peasants, of course), Joachim's horses were startled by the sudden blast of a train whistle, and ran into the locomotive at a level crossing. The door of the carriage had somehow become jammed, so that he was unable to jump clear. Artemis was told that he had been killed instantly, and his embalmed body was placed beside those of his forebears in the marble vault at Horn.

IX

Tamara put Margot's manuscript aside at that natural break. She undressed to go through her usual routine of exercises, musing about the incidence of carriage accidents and whether they had accounted for proportionately as many victims as motor cars. The coincidence of carriage accident and locomotive must have been less common, and not hard to organise. Tamara moved on to the nightly ritual of splashing her face with alternate shocks of hot and cold water. It was tempting to imagine Artemis von Horn, ghostly in white muslin, flapping her draperies at a pair of nervous horses; but unlikely — Artemis would have been as convinced as her attendants that such exertion would kill a newly delivered mother. Perhaps, though, her unorthodox history lessons had included tales of ladies appearing at court balls within hours of their confinements, or of others fleeing the vengeful mob with hours-old infants in their arms. Tamara knew that she might well have committed murder in Artemis's circumstances; and there must have been many unnatural deaths that were supposed to be natural or accidental in an era when some domestic tyrant's disappearance offered the only release from matrimony or poverty.

Tamara slept for eight hours, remembered no dreams when she woke, ate her usual breakfast at the usual time

61

and made herself late for work all the same by squandering minutes in unprecedented dithering about what to wear for lunch with Kim Rice. Should her image be casual or sophisticated, expensive or academic? It was a long time since any man had induced such frivolous uncertainty in her. She painted on several layers of imperceptible cosmetics, wore underclothes that were remarkable for what they left uncovered, and pulled on what she thought of as her 'one good dress'. She took it off again and pulled on jeans. Third time, the last, and perhaps the lucky, time, she put on an outfit bought in Italy that obliged its wearer to swagger.

Bicycling to work, Tamara listened to cassettes of spoken Greek and murmured her attempts at the difficult pronunciation. The odd wolf-whistle penetrated the earphones. She went to her office in Fortress House in which, as well as the Royal Commission on Historical Monuments, were housed numerous government departments including Department E (Works) where Ian Barnes had been employed by a Mr Black. It had never sounded like a glamorous posting for a brilliant graduate, but the job's rewards would have been tangible if Ian had lived to collect them, since those who reached retirement from Department E received large pensions, exalted honours and offers of agreeable sinecures.

After Ian's death Mr Black had taken Tamara onto his strength. She realised then how well suited the civil service warren in which she spent her own blameless working life was to the management of a secret organisation. Its overheads could be concealed from curious audit, its visitors unremarked among the others who waved their duplicated passes at the doorkeepers, its boss disguised in bureaucratic anonymity.

It was months since Tamara had been summoned to Mr Black's office. She devoted her time blamelessly and industriously to the Royal Commission. Her involvement with Department E had been an aberration, she told herself, the kind of uncharacteristic adventure likely to befall women who were disorientated by bereavement. It had all been, she decided, a mistake.

From disparate pieces of evidence, archaeologists construct worlds, detectives construct crimes, and spies construct their ingenious analyses of motives and methods. The desire to satisfy the niggles in the mind which many people ignore, is one of the qualities common to all the deductive professions. Today Tamara Hoyland, well fitted for both her jobs, found her thoughts wandering to the Horn Treasure. She forced herself to deal with the day's incoming mail since she insisted on replying to letters on the day they came. 'You're rocking the boat,' a friend in another department told her, but she said that she answered the same number of queries and wrote the same number of letters on any given day as he did, the only difference being that his all began: *I apologise for the delay in replying to your letter.*

By mid-morning Tamara was free to slip round the corner to Burlington House. In the beautiful library of the Society of Antiquaries, surrounded by the comfortable trappings of enlightened scholarship, she intended to track down the original publication of the drawings of the Horn Treasure from which all later accounts had been copied. The publication had been by the University of Paris, in 1862. The anonymous drawings appeared with a disclaimer by the French professor to whom they had been sent. He took no responsibility. It was a period of antiquarian enthusiasm: in England, ladies and gentlemen watched as their workmen howked beakers and bones out of barrows; in Egypt, travellers wrung their hands over collapsing monuments of the remote past. The treasure, allegedly of Charlemagne, had been much discussed and the sketch reproduced in more popular papers. The reigning Prince of Horn, Artemis's brother-in-law, Waldemar, had issued denials and accusations, but he was able to take no revenge until he entered Paris as a member of the victorious Prussian army in 1871, when the luckless Professor to whom the anonymous informant had sent his sketches, already weakened by months of a starvation diet during the siege, found himself the target of personal as well as national reprisals.

Tamara was not the first person to ask for the publication that morning. Yesterday's evening paper lay on the librarian's desk, folded back to show the paragraph about the German exhibition circled in red ink.

'I think Professor Crawford has got it at the moment,' he murmured, pointing to a table by the window where Tamara's friend and former tutor was making rapid notes. Thea Crawford specialised in prehistory, and looked amused at Tamara's whispered question.

'It's for Sylvester,' she whispered back. 'He wanted me to find out what he needed.' Thea's husband, Sylvester Crawford, was a highbrow journalist.

'It isn't your period either, Tamara,' Thea commented.

'I know, but I . . .' An irritated hushing came from the antiquary working at the next table.

'Coffee?' Thea mouthed. Tamara nodded, and Thea folded her notes into a green lizard skin briefcase. She said, 'We'll go across to the Ritz.'

'Surely, the basement of the Royal Academy –'

'You look ritzy today,' Thea said approvingly, and turned her steps firmly towards the hotel when they came down the steps into the courtyard of Burlington House.

Thea herself spent a large proportion of her salary as a Professor of Archaeology at the University of Buriton on clothes and their accessories. She looked like a frivolous woman but was a serious one, and she was one of the few people who knew something of Tamara's connection with Mr Black's secret organisation. In fact, in her uninvolved way, she probably knew more about Tamara than anybody else alive. It was easy to make confidences to someone who was not sufficiently interested to break them.

The two women looked most unlike the usual image of scholarly females. They attracted interested glances as they walked along Piccadilly, and were greeted with ceremony in the hotel, where Thea was addressed by her name.

'You need to have a drink somewhere comfortable after spending hours in a library,' she explained to Tamara. 'And one might as well discuss our subject in comfort.'

Tamara explained her own interest in the Horn Treasure. 'It's pure coincidence that it is coming to London just now. I doubt whether anyone has looked up that old account of it for years.'

'It should help your friend's book sell; though I'd doubt whether this exhibition will draw the crowds as the Egyptian and Chinese ones did. Not spectacular enough.'

'Thea, surely . . . Carolingian regalia?'

'Look for yourself.' Thea had made one of the elegant sketches that characterised her excavation reports. She was one of the few archaeologists who still published her own accomplished lettering rather than the ubiquitous 'Letraset'. Her pencilled stipples and dashes showed a ring, chalice, broken sword and crown. The crown was a broad circlet said to be of silver, studded with irregularly shaped stones and surmounted by a crystal crucifix, containing, allegedly, a fragment of the True Cross.

'It's all portable,' Thea explained. 'The crown's hinged into sections to fold up, and the chalice probably had its own travelling case. Easy for some mediaeval vagabond to liberate, don't you think?'

'Especially if he simply wore the sword and the ring.'

The ring was gold, and held an amethyst carved with a man's profile. 'A Roman stone re-set, I suppose,' Tamara said.

'I should say almost certainly. It's very like that piece from St Maurice,' Thea agreed.

The sword was the traditional shape, in chased metal with uncut lumps of malachite and garnet set into its pommel. The jewelled chalice was on a splayed base.

'A Carolingian set of regalia would really be like that. Everything is compatible,' Thea said.

'It also tallies precisely with Artemis's description of what she saw in the vault at Drachenschloss.'

'You should publish that section of the letters. It would make a good paragraph in *Antiquity*.'

'I suppose I could ask Margot Ellice if she'd let me.'

'It is about time you started publishing in national journals, Tamara. You are concentrating on archaeology these days aren't you?'

The question had been delicately put, and was probably justified from someone who had once been in academic authority over her, but Tamara chose to misunderstand it. 'There's no bloke to distract me, if that's what you mean.'

'Since the last man I saw you with was the rather ineffectual Magnus Paull, that's good news. Not that you should stay celibate. Someone better will turn up.'

'It's been two years,' Tamara said. Ever since Ian Barnes's death, Tamara had repeatedly told herself that nobody was indispensable, that Ian would have wanted her to replace him, and that she wanted to do so herself. It is a natural instinct to remember only the good of the dead, and Tamara used to force herself to list Ian's faults. She knew that he had not been perfect. She knew that time and custom might have made them enemies, and that if she had not met him by chance, she would have met and married some other man. But she had not yet managed to feel very passionate about anyone else. She said aloud, 'All the same, Thea, I haven't been celibate.'

'I am glad to hear it. But that wasn't what I meant. How's my old acquaintance Tom Black?'

'I didn't think that was what you meant. But the answer is the same. I haven't set eyes on Mr Black for months.'

'Pity.'

'What can you mean?'

Thea hesitated. She concentrated on pouring more coffee from the silver pot, and split some onto the pink tablecloth. A waiter darted forward to wipe it up. 'Here, Tamara, finish the macaroons. Your figure can take them better than mine. I suppose what I mean is something Sylvester said about you.'

The division of labour in the Crawford family meant that Thea's ideas about other people had usually been derived from her husband. He possessed their share of perceptiveness and intuition. Thea's own thought processes were objective and logical. It seemed to make them a happy couple in a semi-detatched way.

'Sylvester wondered whether you could ever be happy with an uneventful life. He thought once you'd seen some action you would want more of it.'

'Nonsense, Thea.' Yet could it be true? Tamara was achingly reluctant to believe it. Not action, Sylvester, but the men who go with it. She said firmly, 'I just like men of action.'

'All the same . . .'

Tamara asked after the Crawfords' son Clovis. He was in Cambridge writing up his doctoral thesis. She asked after Sylvester. He was writing weekly columns in a highbrow left-wing weekly. She kept the conversation firmly on gossip, as she and Thea strolled back along

Piccadilly. By the time that Tamara was back in Savile Row the morning was over. She went into the cloakroom to repaint her face. She stared at herself in the unflattering light. That deceitful mask revealed nothing. Yet Sylvester Crawford, that observant man, had seen more than the face of a pretty innocent.

Tamara left her bicycle chained to the railings in Savile Row and took a taxi to the Tate Gallery. Waiting in traffic jams, she answered the Crawfords in her mind. But it was true that she had enjoyed using her inadmissible skills on Margot Ellice's attacker. Had that episode been like the whiff of his drug to a reformed addict? She tried to be honest with herself.

Tamara Hoyland had returned from her last assignment for Department E feeling disgusted with herself, a failure in her own, if not in Mr Black's eyes. She had sworn to give up her involvement in secret work, in exactly the same way that she sometimes swore to give up a favourite food on which she had gorged.

But one soon longs for the forbidden taste again. More nourishing and less sinful meals become unenticing.

'There are perfectly satisfactory substitutes,' she said aloud.

The taxi driver said, 'Did you say something, darling?'

'I was talking to myself.'

'First sign of madness, that is. Save it for your bloke.'

But I haven't got a bloke – that's the trouble. I need sex, not violence, Tamara thought.

Kim Rice was as attractive as he had seemed at first sight. He was waiting for her on the steps of the Tate Gallery, but had already booked a table and ordered food and wine, and did not let either the meal or Whistler's murals divert his attention from Tamara.

It's very seductive to be concentrated on, she thought analytically, but took pains to let her own eyes wander

68

around the pretty room, and to ask Kim once or twice to repeat his words.

She drank Chablis and claret. Kim was talking about picture restoration. Mr Black was wrong, she thought. He thinks I'm committed to his underworld.

The flooding of the Arno in Florence in 1965 . . .

Why shouldn't I enjoy myself without strings or suspicion?

Botticelli's Primavera . . .

The trouble with secret work is that it destroys one's spontaneity.

The restored sequence of Fra Angelicos in San Marco . . .

If I fancy a man, why shouldn't I just . . .

The excavations in the crypt of the Duomo . . .

Tamara's hand lay on the tablecloth, and Kim covered it with his. His skin was dry and warm. When she leant closer, she could smell faint verbena.

Coffee was sobering. After the meal Tamara went to run cold water over the pulse points on her wrists, and looked at her reflection, thinking, Be careful, pull back, lay off. But the face that looked back was not that of one who feared experience.

'The picture is in Pimlico, shall we walk?' Kim said.

Tamara had forgotten about the alleged Giotto. Kim took her hand, inside his, into the warm pocket of his coat. 'We are going to see a young man who has set up as a middle man in his own flat. He buys at sales and sells to dealers.'

The painting was on an easel in the centre of a small sitting room whose walls were hung with paintings of soulful madonnas and tortured saints. Kim's eyes did not pause on them.

The seller was jittering with nerves. 'I was ever so glad when you got in touch.'

69

'You buy on spec, do you?' Tamara asked.

'Yes, well, you have to when you are starting. I go to country sales and gamble. That's what it is, gambling.'

'Backing your own judgement instead of the auctioneers?'

'Yes, but of course, country auctioneers! Enough said. All the same, it takes some nerve. That's why I was so relieved when –'

Kim, who had been examining the picture on the easel, interrupted, 'Come and have a look, Tamara. See what you think.'

The painting was of several square shouldered, heavy figures, formed up on either side of a madonna and child. The colours were faded, and there was no frame.

'I wondered, at first, a Cimabue . . .' the young man said. Beside Kim he looked etiolated, only half alive, and with his fluttery movements, and gasping speech, seemed to admit inferiority.

Kim laughed. 'Hardly.'

'No, well . . .'

Tamara was used to identifying and dating objects of antiquity. She watched Kim exercising his similar craft. For a while he stood quite still, looking. Then he moved closer and began to peer at the details on the surface, both with the naked eye and through a magnifying glass. After spending a long time going over every centimetre, he moved round to look at the back of the board on which the holy scene was painted.

'What I thought,' said the seller. 'A Giotto di Bondone . . .'

'Thirteenth or fourteenth century, I'll give you that.'

'And Florentine?'

'Humph.' More silent poring. After a while, Kim said, 'Would there be trouble about an export licence?'

'You'll buy it then?' The young dealer's face was

70

transformed. Kim's own remained dead-pan until he and Tamara were well away. Then he laughed and said,

'Let's celebrate.'

'Do you think you've found something special?'

'My client will think so, and that's what matters.'

'Who is he?'

'An American. He'll pay any money for works of art, it's some tax fiddle. If they have a pedigree, the sky's the limit.'

'That picture didn't have a pedigree.'

'Not yet. I shall have traced it by the time he sees it. I have done a good day's work.'

Tamara did not do a good day's work. In fact, she did not go back to work at all. She took Kim back to her flat, and they stayed there until he said he had to go and meet a potential supplier of some Chinese porcelain.

'But it's early,' she protested. 'Couldn't you stay?'

'Another time. That is – another time?'

She said, 'Yes. Another time.'

But I don't know anything about him, she thought, listening to his light footsteps running down the stairs. I don't even know where he comes from or where he's staying. And then she thought, does it matter? She felt more relaxed and at the same time more stimulated than she had during all the last boring months.

A dealer in fine art. A handsome man. An amusing talker. Do I need to know more? She dressed and re-made the bed. With great speed she polished off two reports she had been working on for weeks, and corrected the proofs of an excavation report describing her work in the Isle of Wight the previous spring. Then she cooked herself a substantial supper, and settled down to finish reading Margot Ellice's manuscript.

71

X

Royal persons are not alone in wanting to avoid those who have experienced sorrows they especially dread for themselves, but they are better able to do so. Like her mother, the Princess Royal did not wish even to consider the possibility of being widowed, and Artemis was not summoned to court in Berlin again. She remained as a member of the extended family of the new Prince of Horn, and her son Heinrich shared the nursery of Waldemar and Ulrike's children, Augusta and her baby brother. Heinrich was not a Prince, and without Joachim to insist on it, Artemis was not called Princess. After a while Waldemar, who claimed unlimited power over the members of his House, announced that she was to be known as the Baroness Artemis von Horn and take precedence after the numerous princesses and countesses who lived with them.

It is clear from her letters that Artemis regretted the relegation only insofar as it affected her son. She did not miss the ceremony herself, or the perpetual company of ladies-in-waiting and maids, or, it seems, her husband. She was totally devoted to her baby, and wrote long paragraphs about his sweetness and brilliance.

During the next two years Artemis must have changed: grown up, in fact. Released from the supervision due to the wife of a reigning prince, she began to educate herself in the library at Horn, and when the household moved to town, she attended lectures by Professors at the University in Berlin, and made friends in a circle that the Princess of Horn could never have entered. It is possible that she was at first introduced to such scholars while she was in attendance on the Princess Royal, though she did not mention them at that time in her letters. But others have written of Vicky's enthusiasm for learning, and how her husband had invited some of his own former professors from the University of Bonn to meet her. They came warily, having heard that the English Princess was a tiresome girl, but were disarmed. The scientist Professor Schellbach records that she ran down the stairs to meet him herself, her hair loose, her dress childish, gushing, 'I *love* mathematics, physics and chemistry.' Other philosophers, historians and classicists followed, all flattered at being asked to talk about their own subjects to royalty, and all treated by royalty to Vicky's usual indiscreet pronouncements about her political views.

Waldemar would not have allowed a member of his family to meet such people, and that is probably why Artemis only mentions them once or twice, in passing, to Clementine. She believed that her letters were read before they left Germany. But memoirs published in later years by others who moved in such circles mention the Baroness von Horn; and Wally Hohenthal, who left Vicky's service to marry an English diplomat called Paget, occasionally refers to a 'Diana', her nickname for Artemis, as being present at gatherings of English people and thinkers. In one of her letters she mentions also Philip Ehrenstamm.

It must have been a schizophrenic life for Artemis. Her own inclinations were liberal, anti-authoritarian and even republican, yet she was living and bringing up her son in the house of one of the reactionary party's most ardent supporters. Waldemar was a close associate of Bismarck, to whom (since he was abroad at this time) Waldemar wrote screeds of exhortation and gossip.

With hindsight we know that Bismarck and his followers succeeded entirely, that in September 1862 the King (Fritz's father, who had by then succeeded to the throne) appointed Bismarck as Minister President; that the King lived to a great old age; that during his long reign Bismarck had complete control, and the liberals, of whom Fritz and Vicky were the

73

figureheads, were impotent; and that by the time Fritz became King, he was a tired, middle-aged man, dumb and dying from throat cancer, who reigned as German Emperor for three months before being succeeded by his son, known to us as the Kaiser.

In 1861, however, everyone supposed that Fritz would soon be on the throne. King William was old, had always had poor health, had escaped several assassination attempts – who could have guessed that he would live to the age of ninety-one? The conservatives feared Fritz's accession, and with even more reason, feared his strong-minded English wife. And some conservatives were not the type of people to await passively the outcome of fate.

Waldemar did not hide his disappointment that Vicky survived the birth of her first child; so young, so small, she might well have died, as so many women then did, in childbirth, and indeed, hers had been an especially frightful confinement during which her husband was warned to abandon hope. But she did live, and Artemis told Clementine some of the comments she had heard.

Having lost her husband, Artemis had lost her status, and often heard things that would have been concealed from her if the speakers had thought she mattered. *I cannot bring myself to repeat the words that were used about the Princess and her family, suffice it to say that all was disrespectful in the extreme, and that some allusions were incomprehensible to me. But I understand enough to know that Waldemar and his friends regret that Prince Frederick William was not set free to marry a German princess.*

It may have crossed Artemis's mind that Waldemar and his associates would take more active steps to rid themselves of the English connection, but the ensuing letters are bland and uncontroversial. So long as Artemis lived in the Prince of Horn's house, she guarded her words. The first letter in which she seems to be candid is dated August 1860. It was written from Berlin, the Neues Palais, where Fritz and Vicky lived, and it opens with the remark that Artemis will be able to send it by messenger along with HRH's letters.

I am so grateful to you, dear sister, in this as in everything, that you

74

suggested to Her Majesty that I should accompany the Royal party to Coburg, for I shall have the pleasure of seeing those who have so recently seen you.

Clementine had herself become a maid-of-honour to the Queen by this time. She was to remain in royal service all her life.

While it is safe for me to write freely I must tell you of my fears. I have heard such dreadful things from Waldemar and his friends. I do believe that they would put an end to the Princess Royal's life if it were in their power, so much do they fear the influence of the Prince Consort and of all things English. My friends in Berlin tell me of the extravagant threats they have heard uttered against her. I think you will have understood that I am acquainted with a circle of scholars and scientists, far from the court, with whose philosophical outlook I am more in sympathy, since they agree with our dear Mrs Lambert – to whom, also, I shall take the opportunity of writing freely. Have you gathered from my hints, dear sister, that among those in whose company I have found enjoyment, has been Mrs Lambert's brother, Mr Ehrenstamm? He is a distinguished political philosopher, and accepted in the most superior academic circles. I am so often reminded by his appearance of his dear sister, and of happier days.

Artemis accompanied Vicky and her family to Coburg in September; they were to meet the Queen and the Prince Consort there. The visit started badly, with the funeral of Prince Albert's step-grandmother; but there followed a positive orgy of royal reunions, and Artemis found that she had most of her time to herself.

I should be perfectly happy in this imposing and picturesque place, were only my baby here with me. But I am anxious for him in my absence. I have to tell you, dear sister, that my anxiety grows lest he is neglected or even cruelly treated, in that house where his status, even his legitimacy, is not recognised, so scornfully do his aunts and cousins speak to him and of him – even the servants are insolent – and he the rightful prince! Such protection as I can afford is quite inadequate, and very soon his understanding will be sufficiently developed for him to become aware of the inferior status awarded him. Oh, could my husband only see how his son is treated in his own house! Ulrike has even dared to doubt the validity of any marriage contracted by a reigning prince outside

75

Germany. Thank God my marriage lines are incontrovertible. But would that I could take the child elsewhere. Even to be brought up as the son of a poor widow must be better than to be always the butt of cruel jokes, and to see his cousins favoured over him. When he is of an age to understand that it is his own inheritance so disdainfully witheld, how it will hurt him – and all the more because he will necessarily see that his poor mamma is the unwitting cause of his suffering. Oh, happy England, where morganatic marriage is abhorrent!

Artemis returned to the theme in another letter. When I see the palaces, the estates, the jewels and silver, all property of the Prince of Horn, and realise that Joachim's only son is to be forever deprived of them, and that Joachim's widow – for I was his wife indeed, though they now treat me as something else – has less to call her own than one of his peasants, I do not know how I am to contain myself. You must know, dear Clementine, how indifferent I am to rank and status, indeed, since I have lived at courts I agree more strongly than I ever did in our youth with Mrs Lambert's derision of all such vanities. I daresay I am as egalitarian, republican and liberal a woman as ever lived, and could I only retire to a humble home with my son and a sufficiency on which to maintain him, I should be the happiest of mortals. I tell you, sister, I suffocate at Horn, and in the other establishments that were my husband's and should be my son's. I have asked Waldemar if he would not make it possible for me to take my baby and live elsewhere. I have even asked Ulrike to intercede for me, but he adamantly refuses all I ask, little though it is. But now I hear that he is to come to Coburg, to pay his respects to Her Majesty – for which his hypocrisy ought to choke him, and I pray for the courage to ask him again for that to which I should be entitled, whilst I am under Her Majesty's protection. Mr Ehrenstamm advises me of the least I should accept. Oh, if only I had the means to return to England and to live in peace and retirement with my little son I should feel that the prison gates my father closed upon me had opened at last.

The Earl of Bessemer had died the previous year, leaving nothing to his daughters, or to anyone else, except debts. When the Queen sent for Artemis at Coburg, she spoke of his loss as a tragedy, and shed ready tears at the thought of Artemis and Clementine as orphans, but neither of the participants in that affecting scene could have believed their

76

own words; certainly, Artemis expressed no grief for her father in her letters. It was the Queen, presumably at Clementine's prompting, who had asked Vicky to bring Artemis to Coburg in her retinue, and the Queen then instructed her daughter to make sure that Artemis came to court at Berlin now that she was out of mourning for her estimable and ever-missed husband. Both the two younger women agreed obediently; but Artemis did not have a chance to ask the Queen to intercede for her with Prince Waldemar, who arrived at Coburg a couple of days before the end of the visit.

My brother is being especially – not to say unusually – agreeable towards me in the presence of the English royal party. Twice yesterday he joined me in the garden where I was sketching, and even admired my work, and enquired whether the Princess Royal intended to go out to paint again while she is in Coburg, and whether I should accompany her. I was able to inform him that it is intended to make an excursion tomorrow for the Prince Consort to show his daughter a spot of which he was fond as a boy, and I am to be in attendance. Waldemar then asked me many other details of the daily lives of the royal party. I daresay that I should be grateful for his attention – I assure you, it is no common event for him to honour me with his conversation.

The next letter was written before breakfast the next morning.

I take the opportunity of pouring out my heart to you here, dear Clementine, while it is safe for me to do so, for my letters from my husband's houses are not safe. Dear sister, I so much regret that I have found no moment when I could try to warn Her Majesty or any other member of the Royal Family, of my fears, of what I fear may be done by Prince Waldemar and his friends. He speaks sometimes so wildly of ridding his country of a menace, that I dread how he may try to achieve his ends. When he is in the company of royalty he smiles and defers, but otherwise, he speaks in terms a criminal might use – indeed, I have seen him speaking to men who look like criminals. I am so afraid that he will perpetrate wild deeds that would be deplored even by members of his own political persuasion. It seems absurd to say so in our modern, sober times, but sometimes I fear for the Princess's very life. I must dare to speak of this later in the morning, when I am to drive out with the royal party.

But the Prince Consort took a four-in-hand out alone. The

Princess Royal had a headache, and decided to remain with her mother in the shade. Prince Albert was driving along a country road when his horses bolted at a level crossing.

Unimpeded by long skirts, as the Princess would have been, Prince Albert was able to jump out, and suffered only superficial cuts and bruises. The household at Coburg was cast into deep gloom, for the Queen could not bear anything unpleasant to happen to her dearest Albert, and Vicky was kept busy for the rest of the day, trying to distract her parents with her baby's antics. Later Queen Victoria noted that he was her comfort, her darling, sweet little love, her cherub, and the blessing of his people.

Before the Prince Consort had been carried back to lie on his valet's bed and have Dr Baly tend his sores, Artemis had met Prince Waldemar in the castle garden. He looked astonished, seizing her arm. *He asked me with such excitement why I was here, had I not attended the Princess on the drive with her papa? When I explained that she was unwell, and had chosen to remain within doors, he seemed shocked and dismayed. I believed then that he felt true sympathy for her suffering. Now, dear sister, I have heard details of His Royal Highness's mishap, and I cannot but recall the circumstances in which my husband died. It is all too easy to claim that horses were startled into bolting by a train whistle, all too easy to attribute bruises to a hard road. If HRH had been in the carriage, as had been intended – not to mention myself – what would not have happened? Who was waiting to watch the carriage overturn, and perhaps finish the work? Clementine, I fear that you will wonder whether I am quite in my senses – but I wonder so much whether Joachim's death was what it seemed – whether, perhaps, another such death was to have occurred today. Alas, tomorrow, the royal parties disperse, and I return to Horn. In October we go to Drachenschloss. I shall not be able to write to you freely. But, dearest sister, I implore you, if I too should die, leaving unprotected my motherless child, remember what I say to you today.*

XI

The little screen showed a middle-aged police constable. Tamara opened the door.

He was sorry to trouble her; hers was the only name that seemed to be available in the context. She had known the lady, according to the records.

'What lady? What records?'

The lady was Margot Ellice, the records were those made by the police when she had been assaulted earlier in the week.

'Yes, I know Margot Ellice,' Tamara said patiently.

Margot Ellice was dead.

'Dead? But she seemed all right yesterday. What happened? Anyway, why have you come to me?'

Jeremy Ellice was out of town, and though his sister may have known where to reach him, the fact was . . .

'Yes, officer, I'm listening. Go on.'

The policeman had reached an age to dislike burdening a girl who might be his daughter with bad news. He suggested tea for Miss Hoyland, and sitting down.

Little does he know, she thought, how much tougher I am than he. 'It's all right. Really. And it is Dr Hoyland.'

Doctors are used to horrors. 'There was a fire, you see, Miss, I mean, Doctor . . .'

No wonder this man had never achieved promotion. He wandered verbosely and periphrastically on. After a few minutes, Tamara said crisply:

'Right. I see. There's been a fire in Hampstead at the Ellices' home, and Miss Ellice died in it. You don't know where her brother is, his van's not there, and the only name known in connection with them is mine. Is that it?'

That was it; and it did not seem worth protesting that she knew hardly more about the Ellices than the police did. Tamara rather thought, in any case, that she would prefer to hear from a slightly more competent officer what had actually happened.

'Very mild for the time of year,' the policeman volunteered, as he followed Tamara downstairs. She made the response due in that litany. 'Should keep the street door closed, really, Miss, I mean, Doctor.' He held it wide for her.

'Somebody always seems to forget.'

'It was unlocked when I came in.'

'It doesn't always close properly.' She gave it a tug.

'Too easy for intruders otherwise.'

'I'm sure you're right.'

Tamara could not face a predictable conversation all the way to Hampstead and said she would come in her own car. Yes, she knew the way; no, she was not too shocked to drive. Yes, she was really sure.

It was a clear, windy night, and the yellow street lights cast vivid moving shadows under flapping awnings and tossing trees, so that there always seemed to be movement in the corner of one's vision.

That house could have been a fire trap, with all those books. Tamara had friends who were neurotic about fires and packed rope ladders in their luggage, though fire had not so far been one of her own particular fears; her own horrors came from less practical stimuli. But the picture in her mind of Margot Ellice killed by fumes and flames was painfully vivid.

80

It turned out that she had not been trapped in the basement as Tamara had imagined. The fire had started in the attic where the body was found.

There was a tiny back room that Tamara had not seen, which had contained, as far as could be told, a table and chair, a mattress filled with polyurethane foam, and some crates of books. The fire had been less disastrous than the police constable had implied, and was brought under control quite quickly, but not before the fumes from the burning mattress had suffocated Margot Ellice. The damage to the lower floors of the house was considerable, but caused more by foam and water than by flame.

Tamara was directed to the mortuary, where she identified Margot Ellice's body. She then supplied reams of information about herself, which was written down by hand to her dictation. She repeated that she had no idea where Jeremy Ellice might be, that she had known nothing about the fire, that she had been at work or at home all day; formalities had to be observed no matter how irrelevant they seemed. No, she did not know where Margot Ellice's former husband was, or even what he was called, nor had she any notion about other next of kin. She had met Jeremy Ellice for the first time when she called on Margot the day before; about fifty, very thin, six feet, curly hair, black going grey and worn rather long, pale complexion, bushy dark eyebrows, very long fingers with a badly bruised nail on the right forefinger.

'You seem to have noticed a lot of detail at the first meeting,' the policeman commented.

When she was free, Tamara drove to the house, and parked as close to it as possible. There was not much to be seen from the outside. The fire had been concentrated at the back of the building. But when she wound her window down, the smell of burning, harsh and strangely

81

unsettling, lingered in the night air.

Jeremy Ellice's van slid into a parking space just before midnight; Tamara watched as he got out and unloaded some cardboard cartons, and carried them to his own front steps. She saw him pull out a key and try to unlock the door, and then step back, puzzled, to survey first the front door itself and then the front of the house. He tried the key in the lock again. Then he went into the front garden and peered through the window, first of the the room on the ground floor, then through the railings down into the basement, though the house was dark and there was nothing he could see. He went back to the door and rang the bell several times and then hammered the knocker, shaking his head and glancing up and down the street. A man came out of the house next door and spoke to Jeremy, who listened without moving as the dressing-gowned arm fell soothingly across his shoulders, and gestures of hospitality were made with the other. Jeremy shook his head and went back to his van. Tamara heard him call something to his neighbour about going to the police station.

He had behaved exactly as one would have expected of an innocent man.

XII

Tamara's mother, nothing if not efficient, had already found and installed a new housekeeper to look after Tamara's grandfather, Count Losinsky. 'She costs rather more than I earn, but it's worth every penny until Margot is well again. I have a job on that I can't possibly leave,' Olga Hoyland had said.

Tamara was given the task of telling the expensive temporary helper that Margot was dead, and of persuading her to stay on until a permanent replacement was found. She went to the flat in West Kensington in her lunch hour. The temporary helper was brisk, brusque and very much on her dignity. As well as unpacking all the niceties of life that had been stored away since the death of Tamara's grandmother, such as lace-edged tablecloths and crystal glasses, she had cleared every last item belonging to Margot Ellice out of the bedsitting room and bathroom. 'You could hardly expect me to live with another woman's things in the cupboards.'

'I suppose not.'

'And such things. Of course I've always wanted everything round me to be nice, and nicely kept. I'm funny that way.'

Agreeing, Tamara thought that the sycophancy of an employer desperate not to hear an employee give notice must exceed any creeping to a boss by a person wanting a job. It was worth it in this case, however. The woman was not to Tamara's own liking, but her grandfather seemed happy enough, looking like a bed-ridden Father Christmas with his white beard neatly combed over the embroidered and monogrammed sheets, and with the old silk counterpane on the bed instead of the washable cover that Margot had rightly said was more convenient.

Neither he nor his nurse seemed particularly distressed to hear of Margot Ellice's death, but, just as Tamara was leaving, the other woman said, with grievance in her voice, that she did not know what she was supposed to do now with Margot's mail.

'There will be executors, I presume. I can't be expected to do anything.'

'Of course not,' Tamara agreed, wondering why not. 'Shall I take it? I can pass it on to her brother.'

Not that there was very much; Margot's mail consisted largely of 'money-back' offers and brochures from mail-order companies for which she must have sent off forms clipped from newspapers and filled in with her address. One ought perhaps to think of junk-mail as the lonely woman's comfort, Tamara thought; nice to know it served some purpose. The only personal letter was in a stiff brown envelope with the letters DDR stamped on the back: German Democratic Republic. Tamara dropped everything else into a litter basket and read the contents of this envelope as she sat in the tube train on her way back to the office.

In reply to your letter of March 5th. ultimo . . . No apology for delay, and perhaps Margot was thought lucky to be given an answer at all, having evidently written to enquire about official records of Artemis von Horn's life. No official records of it could be traced. However, the efficient listing of monuments in the disused graveyards of East Germany enabled the undersigned to provide the information that the name in which the enquirer was interested appeared on a memorial tablet in the burial ground of a church in the region of Suhl, formerly Thuringia. On it appeared the inscription:

Lady Artemis Bessemer, died September 3rd., 1863.
Heinrich Joachim Sigismund Bolko Frederick, son of the above, died September 3rd., 1863.

Assuring the honoured lady of their best attention at all times they remained . . .

So Artemis and her son had died within two years of Joachim's death. They had perished on the same day, and the grave had been marked with her maiden name, as though by that time the Horn family had refused to accept the validity of her morganatic marriage.

Had there been another carriage accident – so called? Had mother and son been incarcerated together in another unused closet until they died of hunger and thirst? It conjured up a horrible picture. But it was hard to believe that this woman who had feared for her own and her son's life, had died naturally on the same day as he. It would be, Tamara thought, a pretty peculiar coincidence.

XIII

Mr Black's mind was exercised by coincidence too.

Tamara's name had popped up on some specially programmed computer, and she was summoned to Department E. Mr Black said severely, 'When the names of my young people are associated with suspicious deaths, I need to know the reason why.'

'Artemis von Horn's death?' Tamara's mind was still fixed on the previous century. But she pulled herself together. This lion's den was no place for historical speculation. It was a bleak cabin, furnished to match Mr Black's ostensible civil service grade. If the filing cabinets had impregnable locks, if the window glass reflected external images to watchers outside the building and muffled sound waves from within it, if daily checks were made for recording devices and the cupboard in the corner contained a sophisticated paper destroyer, still a casual visitor would see no more than the type of room in which dull men pass dull hours between suburban train journeys.

Mr Black was not a dull man. Tamara had come to recognise him as devious, autocratic, subtle, but not boring. He was a patriot, and occasionally a poet.

'Artemis von Horn? The family of the Horn Treasure?' he asked.

'Yes, as a matter of fact. But are you concerned with the

treasure?'

'The exhibition is a political event. One has had to postulate all conceivable hitches. The name has been in my mind.'

'The Germans really are sending it, then?'

'It is to be the *pièce de résistance*.'

'It will cause a good deal of excitement,' Tamara said thoughtfully.

'Of a less measured sort than this, I daresay.' Mr Black's forefinger pointed to a page of that morning's edition of a highbrow weekly. Thea Crawford's drawings of the treasure illustrated an article of speculation by her husband. Tamara glanced down Sylvester's analysis of the political implications of this cultural breach in the iron curtain. 'Oh!' she exclaimed. 'Someone *did* see the treasure in this century!' Sylvester quoted part of an account from the memoirs of a Prussian general who had been in attendance on the Kaiser in 1917, when he lived for a while at Drachenschloss with his military entourage, and insisted on being shown the castle's secret treasure. 'I wonder where it has been since the last war. It couldn't have been left where it always was.'

'I know nothing about the treasure,' Mr Black said.

Tamara explained to Mr Black about Margot Ellice's thesis, and Lady Clementine Bessemer's trunk of letters. 'Do you suppose it legally belongs to the DDR? Perhaps the heirs of the von Horns will claim it.'

'I don't think that we can admit any doubts as to its ownership. The treasure is the property of the East German state.'

'For all practical purposes.'

'For all purposes.' Mr Black leaned back in his chair, his eyes travelling along the line where the ceiling met the wall opposite, as though he were reading off some invisible autocue.

'I suppose it isn't all that important,' Tamara said. 'Crown jewels don't confer crowns these days. In the stories of my childhood, kingdoms toppled with the loss of a king's ring. It was a much simpler world.' She giggled nervously, regretting her words as she always used to with her formidable headmistress.

'Simpler? Hardly. Though the world has always been the playground of unscrupulous individuals with suspect motives and devious methods.'

'Which makes me feel that I'm much better off with unworldly scholarship,' Tamara said, reaching for her bag, and making as though to rise.

'But you seem to have become involved with a suspicious death, Tamara.'

'Margot Ellice's? Is it suspicious? Surely it was an accident?'

'There's the usual story of a faulty heater, of course. Room full of paper, mattress stuffed with a filling that gives off poisonous fumes when it burns, wooden floor – it's a miracle that the whole house and its neighbours didn't go up.'

'Why didn't they?'

'A woman across the road called the fire brigade. She said she had sat admiring the sunset reflected in the windows opposite for ten minutes before remembering that it was a rainy day and she was facing north.'

'Is there any evidence of arson?'

'Not as such, not yet; and your friend was safely out of London early enough to be out of suspicion too. The fire was seen at about three o'clock, though it might have been smouldering for an hour or more before that.'

'I first met Jeremy Ellice the day before yesterday, Mr Black.'

'Yes.'

Yes, that didn't, in itself, mean very much. Forty-eight

88

hours were enough to settle anyone's emotional hash, Tamara knew that. She said, 'I just like him, that's all.'

'And you don't think he is the type to leave a time bomb in his house to burn up his sister and his stock in trade in his absence?'

'Hardly.'

'His books are under-insured, by the way. He would have made quite a big loss if they'd gone,' Mr Black said.

'Didn't they?'

'He told the police that the papers his sister was writing and working on were a total loss, but nothing else.'

'The carbon copy of the first section is in my flat,' Tamara said. 'I rather enjoyed it. I shall be sorry not to be able to read the second part. What bad luck that's all gone too.'

Mr Black sat very still, his hands folded as though in prayer, his upright back not quite in contact with the chair, his chin up. It was not hard to see in him the young Guards officer that he had been forty years before; much harder to recognise a man who had purposely chosen obscurity. But when he spoke again his face relaxed into the nondescript lines that enabled him to pass unremarked in crowds. Nothing about Tom Black betrayed his power except his own face unguarded, and few people ever saw that.

He said, 'Miss Ellice came into possession of some papers. The papers gave her information about the Horn Treasure and the family that owned it. The treasure is being sent here as part of a propaganda exercise by the East German government. The papers have simultaneously disappeared. I see.'

'What do you see?' Tamara asked. 'That the fire was caused by someone who wanted to destroy those papers and the woman who knew what was in them? Why should anyone bother, after all this time? Nothing Margot Ellice found out or wrote could affect the present existence or ownership of the Horn Treasure. Even the present Prince of Horn – if there is one–'

'Joachim von Horn,' Mr Black said. 'A member of an ultra-right-wing nationalist group. Lives in Bavaria. Son of one of Hitler's generals, who managed to kill himself in prison before the Nuremberg trials. Grandson of one of the Kaiser's chiefs of staff. I don't think that the contemporary prince will relish seeing his family treasures used as propaganda by its present owners.'

'He won't have much say in the matter I assume.'

'None. The castle of Drachenschloss is well within the borders of East Germany.'

'It doesn't sound, Mr Black, as though the early history of the treasure or the Horn family can have anything to do with the planned exhibition. And presumably that's what interests you in all this. The only thing I did wonder . . .' Tamara said, hesitating.

'Yes?'

'I suppose that what the East Germans are bringing really is the Horn Treasure?'

Mr Black took a stack of photographs from the drawer of his desk. 'This shows what the East Germans intend to send. It's still very hush, the glory of their treasures is to burst upon an unwary world.'

There was the crown, its softly gleaming silver set with gems, and a broken sword polished free of stains. There was a golden chalice; and the amethyst ring was so vividly displayed that the intaglio face seemed to leap from the shiny paper. Each item looked not like a numinous component of legendary treasure, but a sterile artefact, for popular display.

'There should be a mummified corpse in a crystal casket,' Tamara murmured.

From the same drawer, Mr Black took a booklet which Tamara recognised as a catalogue from Plinlimmon's, the Edinburgh firm of antique and fine art auctioneers.

The book fell open at the middle page, which was devoted to a colour spread of an amethyst ring. A large stone, carved with a man's profile, set in gold filigree, and with a hairline crack bisecting the man's cheek, like a scar.

'Plinlimmon's say that it's offered on behalf of a seller from the south of England who bought the ring at a sale in Devonshire,' Mr Black said.

On the facing page, Plinlimmon's had reproduced the drawing that Tamara had examined in the library of the Society of Antiquaries. Mr Black slid the photograph sent by the East Germans across the table. The two amethyst rings were similar but not quite identical; however, each was equally like the nineteenth-century sketch, but for the fact that the ring offered by Plinlimmon's had the faint hairline across the amethyst.

Tamara said, 'Unless some modern glue or tool was used—'

'There is no way of telling which, if either, is ancient.'

'The only actual likeness is there', Tamara said, pointing at the copy of the sketch.

'Which is of dubious authenticity.'

'There's a flaw in the Plinlimmon's ring,' Tamara said.

'That may indicate that it is a copy made from the sketch, with an imperfect stone,' Mr Black said. 'But the East Germans won't like the competition all the same. Depending on who buys from Plinlimmon's, it could all seem like a calculated political insult, the first time they come here with a major exhibition, due to go on to Paris, Melbourne and New York, with unprecedented publicity, and endless flagwaving. Our masters regard the whole thing as being of great political importance. They will not want rival articles about a rival object.'

'A copy?'

'Or a forgery. Most undesirable.'

'What if the East Germans are sending a forgery?' Tamara suggested. She flicked back to the photograph of the crown. Inset was an enlargement of a feature of the cross, showing a small dome of rock crystal, under which a fragment of blackened wood was set. 'You can get a carbon 14 date from wood.'

'That is said to be a piece of the True Cross.'

'So Artemis von Horn was told when she married into the family,' Tamara said. 'It came with us, her husband said, and we shall go with it.'

Mr Black put the pictures away in his desk. He said, 'The German Democratic Republic is sending the authentic regalia of the Carolingian dynasty for display in the West. It is a gesture of goodwill – the first since the Republic was formed. The repercussions in other spheres, if doubt were cast on their generosity, would be . . . let me say, undesirable.'

'They must be allowed their propaganda triumph?'

'Precisely, Tamara,' Mr Black said.

XIV

The wet straw matting, with its rustic smell, had been lifted and draped over the banisters, and the bare floor boards were covered with books spread out in rows to dry. The air felt steamy, with the gas fire and two paraffin heaters turned full on. Jeremy Ellice was crouched in the far corner of the room, leafing through the books from the shelf behind him. He looked mournful and weary, like a monkey hunching itself away from the heartlessness of the world outside its cage. There was still a vacant patch of floor behind the door. Tamara took a book from the shelf, flicked through it, saw that the pages were crinkled like wet blotting paper, and laid it carefully flat.

'Did any of them escape?' she asked.

'Hardly.'

'Any hope of them drying unmarked?'

'Not much.'

They worked together, Jeremy steadily, and Tamara occasionally diverted by the subject of the volume she had chosen.

Jeremy Ellice was obviously exhausted, having been up all the previous night, and having spent much of the morning being questioned by police and insurance assessors.

'It's lucky I can prove I was miles away. I spent

yesterday morning valuing a library in Gloucestershire, and the afternoon at a sale. Then in the evening some of us had dinner before I drove back.'

'Dividing up the spoil?'

'Dealers' rings are against the law.'

'So they are,' Tamara agreed, looking at his drawn face. Jeremy Ellice was not young or attractive, not, it seemed, one of life's winners. Tamara felt sorry for him, with the horrified pity that is so close to a fear of contagious misfortune.

'Do you actually have any other next of kin? I wondered last night.'

'No. There was just Margot and myself, and we were not very close. I feel badly about it now, though you probably noticed I was annoyed by her when she was alive. Even the work she was doing hasn't survived.'

'There's the carbon copy I took home yesterday.'

'Good Lord. So you did. I had forgotten. Though whether that will be much memorial . . . do you think it's publishable?'

'Not as it stands.'

'Poor girl. Mugged, and then dying in this macabre way, so soon afterwards . . .'

'A horrid coincidence.'

'I suppose it must have been coincidence.'

'What else?'

'I couldn't help wondering.'

'Would anyone have wished her harm?' Tamara asked.

'How would I know? We weren't ever very close. She was five years older and we both went off to boarding school at the age of eight. Then school holidays, you know how it is, we both had friends to stay, or went to stay with them, I don't suppose Margot and I were in the same house for more than a month of each year. Then she married Bill Agnew and lived abroad, usually in such uninviting places that I never went to see them, and our parents were dead by then, so there was no base for her here. We used to meet of course when they came to London, but I could never stand Bill and he disapproved of me. We were at the same school and he thought I was a bad advertisement for it. I should have been something like a captain of industry, or at least a professional man, to please him. And he didn't get on with my wife.'

'I didn't know you were married.'

'I am not, now. My wife's remarried, and they are in Scotland with the children.'

'You have children?'

'Three. They come down in the holidays sometimes. Very broad Scots accents, and a fine superiority to my way of life. They only understand about stalking and skiing and shooting, that kind of thing. They don't really know what you are meant to do with books.'

'How sad.'

'Not at all. They are living their lives at first hand. All my experience has been vicarious. Everything I know has come off a page of print. I could tell the kids the words they should use for their activities, I could make a better stab than any of them at describing what it feels like to be out on the moors with a gun or thigh deep in the river after salmon, but I've never done the things. It's all out of books. I'm over educated. You probably are yourself.'

Tamara thought of the deaths she had caused and the dangers she had undergone. Neither showed on her smooth face. She said, 'That may be true of all archaeologists.'

'It is true of all scholars and all readers. We're all over civilised. All the same, oh Lord, give me first hand experience, but not yet. All this is as much reality as I

95

can take.' He gestured around him.

The wooden planks of the floor were smeared with dust that had turned to mud where the fire fighters had reached it. The stairs leading up to the higher floors had been draped with greyish sheets, and there was a barrier on the second floor landing, marked by a pair of printed labels: EXPOSED POWER CABLES, KEEP CLEAR; and GAS TURNED OFF.

'The forensic people finished here this morning,' Jeremy said.

'How long before you hear from them?'

He did not know, or seem to care. He worked on, occasionally stopping to mourn over a ruined volume, and once or twice to gloat over a precious one. 'Thanks be that the Baskerville Press ones were out of range,' he said piously. Tamara admired his row of leather bound editions of fine printing. 'It took me years to complete this set, and I suppose I should be ashamed of the way I managed it.'

'Did you steal them?' Tamara asked.

'Somebody did. These two were on a stall in the Portobello Market. I bet they were stolen from their owner, they were far too cheap and the book plates had been steamed off.'

'Are they legally yours, then?'

'They wouldn't be if I'd bought them in a shop. Title in stolen goods doesn't pass to a purchaser, no matter how innocent, unless they are sold in an open market.'

'Market Overt?'

'That's right. English law seems to be riddled with mediaeval phrases. It has to be a long established market place, out of doors I think. I suppose the idea was that the owner might have a chance to claim his own goods back in time if they were displayed there, before anyone else had a chance to pay good money for them.'

'That might have worked in a mediaeval village, I suppose.'

'Yes, it's crazy now, isn't it? But lucky for me.' Jeremy rubbed his thumbs affectionately over the glossy leather, and showed Tamara the handsome title pages. But there was hardly an inch of flat surface left to arrange the damp volumes on.

'Let's stop for a while. Come on down.'

The stairs were puddled with stains and footprints, but the door of the basement room was tight fitting, and must have been closed the previous day, for the room looked unchanged since Tamara had last seen it, except that the bed was unoccupied, and covered with a gaudy mirror-work cloth.

'Amazing how little trace there is in here,' Jeremy said. But Margot's suitcase was still on the chair beside the bed, its lid open to show her sensible nylon dressing gown, and plastic hairbrush, and on the bedside table were the books about nineteenth-century court life that Jeremy had brought her. Tamara opened the letters of Queen Victoria and her daughter, the Princess Royal, at the page where Vicky had written about her ladies-in-waiting.

They are so very nice, the more I see of them the more I love them, they are so full of tact, and always so respectful and nice to me, they are more like sisters than anything else.

Jeremy made tea. It was evidently a ritual, the pot polished, the tea precisely measured, the cups warmed, an incongruously elegant ceremony for those filthy hands to perform. He said, 'I keep wondering whether it might have been more than an accident, I know those paraffin stoves are supposed to be dangerous, but I can't think why it should have toppled over, and even if it did, why the papers Margot was working on, and very little else, should be gone.'

'What do you mean, Jeremy?'

'I can't help thinking that Margot might have started the fire herself. I don't mean that she wanted to commit suicide, but perhaps she had some reason for wanting to destroy those papers, and lost control. Not that I can imagine what it was.'

'Is there a fireplace in the room?'

'Just a tiny disused grate with a mini-mantelpiece, not big enough to heat the room. It hasn't been used since I lived here. But Margot might have lit the papers from the flame in the paraffin stove, meaning to put them in the grate to burn, and somehow knocked it over.'

'Why do you suppose that Margot would have wanted to destroy her research material? Those papers were her dowry, that's the word she once used to me,' Tamara recalled. 'She said they were her passport to the academic world. She was going to make a contribution to knowledge that would establish her as a serious historian.'

'You don't think there could have been something that disgusted her so much that she wanted to be rid of it at once?'

'Or frightened her?' Tamara suggested. They sipped tea, together, thinking about Margot's work.

Jeremy said, 'It could hardly be anything to do with the death of Artemis von Horn and her son. Even if it was murder, it's so long ago . . .'

'It's the kind of skeleton people are quite proud to find in their cupboards. Romantic, wicked ancestors. Anyway, with a Junker General and a Nazi nasty in the family tree, a little thing like a forefather who murdered Artemis wouldn't worry anyone,' Tamara said.

'I didn't know about them.'

'I looked them up, didn't I mention it?' Tamara told him. 'I found out more about the treasure too.'

'Ah yes. The priceless treasure.'

'It would be priceless, literally. How could you put a figure on it? Tamara's training and temperament did not lead her to think of such things in financial terms. The least important of the attributes of the Horn treasure, as far as she was concerned, would be its cash value. She took a pencil and paper from the mantelpiece, and quickly made a drawing for Jeremy of what the treasure looked like.

'All those jewels . . .' Jeremy murmured. 'It's positively vulgar.'

'To mediaeval eyes they would have been intoxicating, a foretaste of heaven's splendour. Each stone had its own mystical significance, you know,' Tamara said.

'It is really a symbol of the misuse of wealth and power,' Jeremy mused.

'A very anachronistic view,' Tamara replied severely. 'Poor down-trodden peasants couldn't eat precious metals or stones, obviously, or do anything else useful with them either. The sight of them would have been cheering.'

'Bread and circuses.'

'Exactly as television is now. Something bright to look at, something to take your mind off present gloom and problems. Looking at these things would have given people an idea of how nice it would be in heaven.'

Jeremy stared disapprovingly at Tamara's drawing. 'It's all sociologically deplorable,' he said. 'And in any case, I don't see how the Carolingian crown jewels found their way to a secret vault in Thuringia. Wouldn't they have been needed for some coronation or other? Not that I can see why anyone cared. Perhaps I'm lacking in historical imagination.'

'It seems possible,' Tamara told him, 'that this lot could be the third set of Imperial regalia – the Holy

Roman Empire, that's it. We do know that the later emperors used to be crowned three separate times, once in Rome, once in Lombardy and once in Aachen. Two of those crowns are in museums. If this is the third, it could have been the booty of some mediaeval brigand. That would be perfectly plausible. Actually, Jeremy, I'm thinking of writing a Note for *Antiquity* about it, quoting Artemis's authentic description of the treasure in situ. I wish her letters hadn't gone. Will you testify for me that it really existed? You'll have to give me some details about where you found the trunk they were in.'

'As I told you, I picked up Clementine Bessemer's trunk at a sale in Devon. It was a house that was being sold up, about to be demolished I think. They were digging away the land for china clay around there. So it was one of those auctions where you find everything: chamber pots, family portraits, unidentifiable gadgets, photograph albums – lots of those.'

'I know those old albums. There's something very poignant about them,' Tamara said. 'Brown snaps curling away from cellophane corners, with white writing. Lots of forgotten names and faces.'

'They are not the sort of thing I'd buy,' Jeremy said.

'Of course not.'

'And I don't know who did buy them,' he went on. 'But I did look through one or two. Now, there was one snap I remember, a set of kids posed all over a garden, in fancy dress costume.'

'Oh how I hated fancy dress parties!'

'This must have been before the war.' He screwed his eyes closed trying to visualise what he had seen. 'A woman in a sort of belted sack with a hat pulled down to her eyebrows.'

'A cloche.'

'And buttoned shoes, pointed, with a cross bar.'

'That would be in the nineteen-thirties.'

'Yes, a fancy dress party in the thirties, with pictures of the children posing about – the sort of thing I went to myself.'

'What about it, Jeremy? That's what you'd expect to see photos of in an old album.'

He said slowly, 'There was one kid I remember, two or three of the pictures were of him. Posing alone for a camera, once on a sort of platform thing, like an upturned waggon, and then another sitting in a great chair with arms like a throne, and one with a pony. There was a man in the picture too, what was it . . . ?'

'Does it matter?' Tamara said impatiently.

'It might, yes. Because you see, I remember what the little boy in the photographs was wearing. He was dressed up as a king. He was holding a sword, broken, but still long, and too heavy for him so that it trailed on the ground; he couldn't have played games with it, just held onto it for the photograph. And he had a crown on.'

'I daresay he did, if he was dressed as a king. I used to dress up as a queen in a crown, too.'

'The crown was too big for him, too. It was down over his forehead. He had very short hair, which stuck up inside the crown in a sort of tuft. You could see that he would take the crown off the moment the camera clicked. They were rather good pictures.'

'So?'

'The crown was a circle, with lumps on it that must have been jewels.'

'Pretend jewels, presumably.'

'They caught the light. You could see that in the snapshot, the sun reflected off them. And there was a crucifix sticking up in front. Just like your drawing, Tamara, just the same.'

'I suppose the child was wearing a ring and carrying a

chalice,' Tamara said sceptically.

'I can't remember . . . no. He couldn't have been. The ring would have been far too big.'

'Just what are you suggesting, Jeremy?'

'I think I may have seen a photograph of the Horn regalia, the Treasure.'

'Very likely, I must say! – worn as fancy dress in rural Devonshire in the nineteen-thirties!'

'I have a good visual memory. You need it, in my profession.'

'Crowns and swords all look much the same,' Tamara said. 'It's what archaeologists call functional stasis.'

Jeremy Ellice was pacing up and down the long room, stepping aside to avoid furniture with practised ease. A track was worn across the matting, like a cow-path across a field. As he moved, he automatically adjusted the books that lay on every flat surface, sometimes picking one up to carry to another table on the other side of the room, sometimes pausing to stroke a binding or glance at a title page. He said, 'You know, Tamara, if the Horn Treasure had been stolen from that dungeon . . .'

'From an impregnable castle in its lonely mountains?'

Jeremy picked up the books on the bedside table. 'These are the books I got for Margot. I must put them in the shop.' A white card floated to the floor and he bent to pick it up.

Tamara said, 'If Artemis took the treasure herself and passed it on to someone else –'

'Who could have brought it to England and passed it on to Clementine Bessemer, so that it was with her other belongings in Devonshire –'

'But that can't be right. It was seen at Drachenschloss in 1917. By the Kaiser, at that.'

'Anyway,' Jeremy said, 'why should Artemis have taken it?'

'She might have thought she had a right to take it, for her son. She was convinced that he was his father's rightful heir.'

'That idea of morganatic marriages is very unpleasant to our generation, isn't it?'

'Just as distasteful as the idea of marrying for money,' Tamara agreed.

'How do you think Margot got hold of this?' Jeremy Ellice exclaimed, reading the words on the card he had picked up. '*Joachim, Prince of Horn*, it says.'

Tamara took it from him. The name was engraved in copperplate. Pencilled underneath were the words, *London Lodge Hotel*. She said, 'That will be the present prince, not Artemis's husband.'

'Oh I see, of course. Where do you suppose . . . Margot didn't mention him. Do you suppose she wrote?'

'She probably asked for any information he could provide, it's the usual thing to do. It was in the books you bought Margot about Court life.'

'I hope I shall be able to shift them. Margot seemed so keen to acquire them that I plunged a bit.'

'I suppose they are outside your usual field – like photograph albums.'

'I probably should diversify,' Jeremy said gloomily. 'I certainly shan't get rich at this rate.'

'Into costumes, for instance?'

'What do you mean?'

Tamara said, 'I was wondering about that sale you went to in Devon. Would you have noticed if the dressing-up gear you saw in those photographs had been on sale, too? I mean, a crown, or a sword or anything?'

'I always look at the mixed lots. You never know, country auctioneers can make idiotic mistakes. But one could hardly overlook a set of crown jewels.'

'I just wondered whether they could conceivably still

103

be there,' Tamara said.

'You mean, if Artemis really did make off with them, and they really were in Devonshire in the nineteen-thirties? Perhaps they are, just waiting to be found. Waiting to make someone's fortune.'

Tamara looked at his gaunt but suddenly eager face. Annoyed with herself, she said, 'They wouldn't be, of course. It was a silly idea. Even if they ever were there, they would have gone for scrap in 1940. It was only a passing thought.'

XV

London Lodge was not listed in the motoring handbooks or the *Michelin Guide to the British Isles*, being deficient in plumbing, car parking spaces and television sets. The Prince of Horn perhaps made his choice out of the *Good Hotel Guide*, which described it as an agreeable oasis of eccentricity in an increasingly standardised desert of sanitised hotels, and an original experience for unstuffy visitors.

The rooms had no telephones, and the proprietor's baby tended to disturb the guests, but the views of the Thames were spectacular, the furniture valuable and the food unique. Tamara had more than once been taken to dinner in the 'heliotrope-scented conservatory tactfully converted into a dining room', and knew where to find the alley that led from the outside lavatories into the residents' lounge; she also knew that the set dinner was served at eight o'clock, and that the tyrannical owner would banish from his premises any customer who was so disrespectful of the food as to smoke, disagree with his choice of wines, or leave the room during the meal.

Tamara crossed the lounge, where Crown Derby coffee cups were already set out on a low stool in front of a log fire. In the dining room, guests shared a single oval table and were served by waiters dressed as butler, footman and parlourmaid. The proprietor always took the head of the table and discoursed on the seasonings and garnishes as different dishes were carried on silver platters for the company to admire. Through the lounge door, Tamara saw a procession of servants on their way to make sure that each person at the table simultaneously received a miniature soufflé arising out of a pastry mould. A delicious aroma of smoked fish followed them; there would be several more courses still to come.

All the dinner guests assembled for sherry (cocktails being forbidden, since they spoiled the palate for fine wine) before dinner; it must have been at that time that the girls, who later changed into black dresses with white frilly caps and aprons, rushed around the bedrooms in their pink prints and mob caps to turn down the beds, for when Tamara let herself into the Prince of Horn's room she found a banked-up fire burning in a polished grate, an invitingly turned-back linen sheet on the four poster bed and a pair of pink silk pyjamas laid ready on the chaise longue. The room was decorated in full Victorian style, down to the basin and ewer on a stand in the corner; for use, not decoration. The hotel's bathroom was magnificent, but there was only one. A copper kettle was warming on a brass trivet beside the fire, and a curved mound at the foot of the bed showed that a stone hot water bottle had been inserted. The several tables in the room were covered with lace cloths, and bore numerous small china ornaments and posies of everlasting flowers.

Incongruously modern in this revivalist setting, a black leather briefcase was lying on an embroidered footstool. It was fastened by a combination lock. 'The briefcase hasn't been invented that I couldn't open in ten seconds and you lot in ten minutes,' the instructor at the house in Bayswater had boasted. Tamara had been a star pupil at that particular skill. The Prince of Horn's

106

case took one and a half minutes to open.

It contained a stack of papers: a copy of the original edition of the drawings of the Horn Treasure, published in Paris in 1862; a sale catalogue from the house in Devon where Lady Clementine Bessemer's trunks had been sold, with the number of that lot circled in red ink, and several unattributed paintings underlined; a formal letter from Margot Ellice wondering whether the present Prince of Horn could help her in her research, its address Paul Losinsky's west London apartment; and a photocopy, pale grey paper with only slightly greyer type, of Margot Ellice's work, both the first part, of which Tamara had read a copy, and the second.

The second part was short. As her work progressed, Margot Ellice had either decided to let Artemis's own words speak for her, or had not yet had time to transpose them into a third person narrative. Large chunks of the letters were copied in Margot's accurate typing.

Artemis had returned from Coburg to her son and her husband's family. She wrote from Drachenschloss with great caution, frightened that her words would be quoted by those who spied on her, and much of her letters consisted of innocuous accounts of the weather, the scenery, and Heinrich's amusing behaviour.

That winter, two professors from the University of Bonn visited the Castle to study its antiquities and report on them to Prince Frederick William, who had learnt to take an interest in such things from his cultured wife and her father, the Prince Consort. The Family of Horn was much displeased at this impertinent intrusion, but a Prince of Prussia's wishes were obeyed by even the haughtiest noblemen, in marked contrast to the indifference that Prince Albert's advice had evoked in the late Earl of Bessemer. Prince Waldemar of Horn had felt obliged to agree that Professor Gottfried and Mr Ehrenstamm should be admitted to the vault at Drachenschloss under the outraged eye of the Chamberlain.

Naturally, dear sister, the two gentlemen do not stay in the Castle. I believe that they put up in a village some five miles distant, and they are of course not received by their serene highnesses. I have been able to exchange some words with them, for I have more freedom from supervision since I am no longer the wife of a reigning prince, and am seldom accompanied by attendants. My movements, I believe, are a matter of indifference to the Family.

Artemis made use of her freedom. One night, having been excused from dinner on account of a headache, she and her son left the castle of Drachenschloss. The next letter was dated January, 1860.

Hotel du Parc, Versailles.

My dearest sister, I write to acquaint you with the news that I have this day been united in matrimony, in the deepest secrecy and concealment, with my dearest Philip. This letter comes to you from France as you see, but we shall not breathe easily, nor cease to fear vengeful pursuit, until we are on the shores of my own dear country that is to be Philip's adopted home, the land of liberty and justice.

So how had she died that April in Thuringia? Gripped by the story, Tamara read eagerly on.

I count the moments until I can embrace you and present to you my beloved son. Henry is already on the happiest of terms with his new papa, and with his aunt, our own dear Mrs Lambert, whose name we intend to take as our own the better to conceal our whereabouts from those who may come seeking Artemis or Heinrich von Horn, or Artemis Bessemer, or Philip Ehrenstamm.

So Artemis had married Jeanette Lambert's brother, the young Jewish philosopher. Philip Ehrenstamm, Philip Lambert – it came to Tamara that she knew the name. It swam to the surface of her mind from the buried depths of her history studies at school: Philip Lambert, author of *Meditation au sujet des philosophies politicales*, in two volumes, published some time in the eighteen-eighties.

My only regret, dear sister, is that by this deed Philip has cut himself

*off forever from his own father and family in Berlin. We two, and dear
Jeanette, and you and our son, shall be all in all to each other.*

Would Clementine have been any better pleased at the
introduction of a Jew to her aristocratic family, than the
Ehrenstamms at their Philip 'marrying out'?

*A new and happy life awaits us far from the tyrannous whims of
princes or autocrats, in the free shores of my own country. We have fled
like fugitive criminals from the place over which my son should rightfully
reign. In time I shall tell you of our hazardous journey. Let me now
merely say that my dear Philip was waiting for us at the rendezvous we
had agreed, when we crept from the Castle at dead of night, never to
return before my son comes into his own again. I brought with me only the
merest necessaries, packed, along with a token of my son's rightful
property, into two bags. We have been forced to sell the little jewellery
left me (since Prince Waldemar claimed most as family heirlooms) in
order to finance our travels, and God willing we shall arrive in England
within the week.*

Her son's rightful property? Had Artemis von Horn
taken Charlemagne's treasure from the vault before
leaving Drachenschloss for ever? She believed that it was
her son's by right. She would not have thought that
she was stealing. Tamara wondered whether Philip
Ehrenstamm would have taken the jewellery to his
father's shop; but no. The first place the von Horns would
have begun the search for their missing treasure would be
any establishment connected with the professors who had
been permitted to see it.

What must Philip Ehrenstamm have thought when he
discovered that Artemis had brought the treasure with
her? He would have been horrified, probably, but
lumbered, and as determined as the von Horns to keep it
secret that the treasure was no longer in the vault. And
then his scholar's conscience would have driven him into
making sure that a permanent record was published; but

109

when Professor Duvallier at the Sorbonne received the anonymous drawings, he, like everyone else, would have supposed that they were records of a collection that remained where it had always been.

Dear Clementine, I am sure that you will believe my assurance that I have taken only that to which my son is entitled. Subterfuge is forced upon us, but might is not right.

Of course Artemis would not have been able to take her place as a Bessemer on her return to England. The von Horns would have been over there within days of her disappearance, looking for their treasure.

Once Waldemar found that she and her son were not to be traced, he announced their deaths. But then – perhaps they had been recovered, and had died. For the treasure had returned to Drachenschloss – or, if it had not, what was it that was due to be displayed in London?

It was easy to see why Artemis had eloped, and it would not simply have been for love of Philip Ehrenstamm. She must have feared another carriage accident like that in which her husband had died, or the one in which the Prince Consort had been injured; and she wished to protect her son. No doubt Artemis believed what her husband had told her, that an enlightened King, spurred by his English wife, would see that the restrictions on the rights of the children of morganatic marriages would be lifted. Artemis must have supposed that Waldemar feared being dispossessed and regarded Heinrich's life as a threat.

When my son comes into his own again I shall return. Until that time, he is safer as Henry Lambert, a commoner, hiding from those who have stolen his birthright; and safer too, hidden by my sister and by my namesake at Stockwell, are those precious proofs that are his right, for of those, too, I believe my enemies would deprive me, dishonouring my name, and that of him who gave it to me.

Heinrich von Horn, Henry Lambert, could never have

110

come into 'his own'. Artemis could not know, nobody then could have guessed, that the enlightened Frederick William, after waiting thirty years for his throne, would die within weeks of ascending to it, having spent the whole of his career as the impotent, ignored opponent of his father's reactionary regime. Murderous hotheads like Waldemar could afford to leave Vicky unmolested. Under Bismarck there was no time or place for liberalism, and among the many reforms that never took place, was the abolition of morganatic marriages and their consequences.

Artemis's escape to England was followed by epistolatory silence. Perhaps she lived in England and was able to speak instead of writing to her sister. Very soon after the date of Artemis's departure from Drachenschloss, Queen Victoria mentioned in her diary the presence of Prince Waldemar in England, and on the same day she refers to sending her personal physician, Sir James Clark, to call on Lady Clementine Bessemer to make sure that the ailment keeping her from court was not infectious. One may infer that Clementine was taking care to avoid Waldemar's questions.

The next letter in the collection was dated two years later from a ship on which the Lamberts were crossing the Mediterranean.

The sea air and brilliant sunshine are indeed causing my wretched health to improve.

Artemis notes, amid her eulogies of the scenery and flora.

I breathe more easily, and it is some days since I have coughed blood. Henry thrives on the life at sea. How different is this happy childhood, in the company of two loving parents, and the affection of his two dear aunts, from our solitary life at Stockwell, strangers to our parents as we were. Henry makes friends with all the world, sailors, servants, other travellers, and he already converses in three languages.

Next comes an account of a day on the shore in Sicily,

with much gushing emotion at the sight of a ruined temple.

My life in Germany is like a bad dream vanished with the dawn, and in the shared charge of the Huntress and her sister rest its waking traces.

Artemis's language had become more flowery and high flown since she married her philosopher.

We shall live, dear sister, in the remembrance of those who loved us; that is what my husband teaches me.

Artemis died of consumption when the ship was somewhere between Cyprus and Palestine. Philip Lambert told Clementine that Henry would be his own son whose father's care would never falter, and he closed his melancholy account of every cough and haemorrhage with warm expressions of fraternal devotion to Clementine Bessemer. Artemis's body, he wrote, was committed to the water.

That was the end of Margot Ellice's patchwork history. Tamara slid the papers back into the briefcase, and began to unfold the next document. She had been too fascinated by the story unfolding on those smooth grey pages to pay proper attention to what was going on in the hotel. Now she realised that the soothing murmur of cooking and eating in the distance was the background to fast, firm footsteps coming along the passage.

There was no room between the bedsprings and the floor for a human being. None of the tables was large enough for Tamara to be concealed below its dangling cloth. Moving quickly, she pushed the flap of the briefcase so that it would appear closed to a casual glance, and stepped into the central section of the large tripartite mahogany wardrobe. She cowered in pitch darkness among the suits and coats, and listened to the door of the room open, and masculine steps entering. Tamara could see nothing except a narrow line of light around the edge of the door. If he had come to fetch another jacket, or the anorak against whose smooth nylon Tamara was resting her cheek . . . steps came in her direction. I shall pass myself off as a practical joker, she thought; say that his friends had arranged for him to find me naked in his bed when he slid his toes down to that hot stone bottle. Or should I burst into song? In the London of the nineteen- eighties there are so many loony possibilities, from singing telegrams to iced cakes bursting open to reveal four and twenty singing black girls, that I ought to get away with it. If he's middle-aged he should be pleased. If he's young he might laugh. Otherwise . . .

The wood of the cupboard, like a sounding board, magnified the squeak when the left hand door opened, but the whole structure was so well made that it did not even tremble. Pinching her nose to avert sneezes, Tamara listened to a pair of shoes falling onto the ground, and another being lifted from the cupboard. She could almost hear the scraping of fabric as the laces were tied.

He shut the door and walked away. He paused. Had he noticed that his case was unfastened? No, he was leaving the room. The door slammed and its key turned.

When Tamara stepped out of her hiding place, she was surprised to find that she was still holding a couple of sheets of paper in her trembling hand. I used to be cooler, she thought, but with trained thoroughness paused to read them. One was a sheet of working drawings, a jeweller's blueprint for the accurate reproduction of the Horn Treasure. Here was a plan for the crown, chalice, ring and sword, and the sketch of the completed objects seemed identical to that published in 1863. There was a signature in the corner, in tiny letters: *V. L Volkersheim, 1917*.

Tamara had read, but never quite taken in the extent to which it was possible for the rich upper classes in Britain and in Germany to live as though their world were not coming to an end over there in France's trenches, during the first world war. That a jeweller could have supplied

113

the materials, the skill and the time to create a replica of the Prince of Horn's lost treasure in 1917 was a chilling little piece of evidence.

Waldemar must have known that the treasure was gone for good. Presumably he had done nothing more about it, apart from ceasing his family's annual ceremony of worship in the vault, until his all-powerful Emperor had announced his intention of seeing it in 1917. Certainly those who had acquired that replica by conquest in 1945 could have had no idea that it was not the original treasure. It was probably a piece of secret information, handed down from father to eldest son in the family.

The last piece of paper was a sheet of foolscap showing a rough draft of a letter with many changes and erasures. Some sentences were in English, some in German. *A crude deception foisted upon a credulous world . . . political advantage derived from fraud . . . expose the crude forgery now being forced upon willing dupes . . .*

The contented sound of heavy eaters enjoying their coffee and brandy was floating up from the lounge. Tamara tidied her ruffled appearance, using some of the powder provided for women guests and the Prince of Horn's comb. She re-locked the case on all its papers, and put it where she had found it on the chaise longue. On the stairs she met an elderly American who had dined unwisely and too well, and she waited at their foot while the hotel's owner crossed the hall and closed the door of his office behind him. She was sorry not to set eyes upon the Prince of Horn among the men clustered round the wood fire. He had presumably changed his shoes in order to go out, and none of the jovial, flushed diners could possibly be he. It was a pity. Tamara would have liked, just once, to see him.

XVI

In her parents' house Tamara, the youngest of four children, would always be treated as such; cherished, teased, admired, but never taken quite seriously as an adult. Arriving there, she felt responsibility sloughing off, an agreeable immaturity regenerated. She did not really regret having refused Kim Rice's pressing invitation to accompany him on a detecting trip. He wanted to trace the pedigree of the picture he had bought. Tamara had told him that she had to go home for a long weekend. 'I shall miss you,' he said, and she felt the tickle of excitement at the prospect of their next meeting.

It was not a woman who knew more than her family ever could about violence and deception who entered their large, untidy hall; it was not the secret agent who had once caused two terrorists to die in their own explosion who threw her coat onto a chintz sofa; not the outsider who had once kept a traitor from high office who called 'Anyone at home?' into the warm silence. The girl who rushed into her mother's embrace was still dependent on that mother's approval; she hugged a father she could bend to her will; she kissed a sister with whom she would always feel competitive and in whose older face she could see a prophecy of her own.

'You girls are still absurdly alike,' Mrs Hoyland said fondly, but Alexandra pulled back, shaking hair from her eyes, and said,

'Not any more. I'm covered with wrinkles.'

'What nonsense . . .'

But Alexandra had left the room. The change had been very recent, from the younger sister striving to emulate a glamorous elder, to Tamara's new state, of being envied by Alexandra.

'The children wear her out, poor thing,' Mrs Hoyland said, and Tamara nodded. She might have had children herself by this time, if Ian Barnes had lived. Tamara's mother and father noticed details of her appearance, as though from it they could guess whether she had yet found a replacement. Neither of them had ever said that they would like her to settle down to conventional life, in fact, far from it; for both had always been delighted by her academic successes and professional status, but she knew that they both hoped she would marry. Tamara herself had long since outgrown any rebellion against her parents' standards. She too would have liked to get married and have children. But the men she had found since Ian's death had not been imaginable husbands, and she knew that even Ian himself would have been a bad bet; only a fool would plan a peaceful life with a secret agent.

Kim Rice's lover did not feel like a secret agent; archaeology, antiques and art, she thought alliteratively, would offer greater lifelong satisfactions.

Alexandra recognised the secret smile of a younger sister. She asked the question no parent would dare to put. 'Who is he this time?'

'Who?' Tamara said.

'Whoever it is that's making you look like a cat that got the cream.'

Rob Hoyland was used to making peace between his children. He closed the book that Tamara had brought

116

him, a long sought edition of one of David Lindsay's esoteric fantasies, and said, 'I have been hunting this for years. Where did you find it?'

'I am afraid it's a bit damaged. It's from Jeremy Ellice.'

'Ah yes, poor man. So sad about his sister.'

Rob Hoyland made room in the bookcase for his new acquisition. All the Hoylands bought books. They lay in piles on every table, and were stacked on window sills and beside every seat in the house, including the lavatory. They competed for wall space with the pictures, whose number increased with similar speed. The Hoylands' house had been designed in the eighteenth century for a more formal pattern of life than that to which it had been adapted. Smaller rooms with separate functions had been joined together, so that the ground floor now consisted of a square entrance hall, furnished with seats and a mahogany table covered at most times of the year with flowers; at present it carried a dozen varieties of cyclamen. On either side of the hall were two very large rooms, one a library cum drawing room, the other a kitchen-dining-sitting room. Both were full of the choices of two catholic tastes, paintings, drawings, pottery, ornaments, oriental rugs, contemporary weavings and complicated mechanisms for playing music. Each item had been chosen for itself, and no limit had been set to the number of patterns or periods of manufacture. When the Hoylands were in a bad temper they complained that the place looked a mess. When they came home from the outside world, it felt like a sanctuary.

It was unprofessional of me to come home, Tamara thought, her mind slithering into contentment; I should have stayed in a commercial travellers' hotel. She had never been able to concentrate on her work here, in spite of the parental encouragement, but had always returned to her university during vacations when she had to study.

'I suppose you're going to tell us you have been working hard,' Alexandra said, settling her children round the table. She tucked one into a high chair, another onto a cushion, and took the youngest on her knee. 'Wait until you have tried this game, then you'll know what hard grind really is. It's like a treadmill.' But as she spoke her lips were nuzzling the soft nape of her baby's neck. Tamara watched the combined exasperation and devotion with a painful kind of interest.

'I can see that they take up all your time,' Tamara accepted a plate from her mother. 'What elaborate food. Weren't you at work today?'

'Mother doesn't cook any more,' Alexandra said. 'The deep freeze gets filled by a freelance. It's the modern equivalent of the kitchen staff.'

'Sandra's been busy, too; she's organising an appeal to keep some pictures in the county,' Rob Hoyland said.

'Yes, you should be interested in it, Tara,' Alexandra said in a more friendly voice. She gave herself and the baby alternate mouthfuls, occasionally pausing to re-direct the middle child's spoon. 'Two Gainsboroughs and a Turner, they were sold at Sothebys to an American but we're hoping to get an export licence refused if we can raise the cash to buy them back. They ought to be here in Devon, not even in London. The big national museums have enough loot, we need them here. Father should have done something about it at the time.'

'My dear, you know we had to raise as much money as we could. I had no discretion in the matter. Only the pictures that the man from the National Gallery said were unimportant could be sold down here.'

'That's all very well, but James says—' Alexandra's husband was a lecturer at Bristol University. He was a

118

man of startling good looks and equally startling dullness. Tamara had never yet found a single subject on which she could sustain a conversation with him for more than three minutes, although he was professionally concerned with conservation and the environment, both topics that interested her. Even when Alexandra quoted him Tamara's ears almost involuntarily switched themselves off.

When her voice stopped Tamara said, 'I didn't know you had been involved in the sale at Stockwell, Father. I came across something the other day . . .'

'We act for the beneficiaries.'

'Parasites,' Alexandra hissed.

'Expatriates,' her father said. 'They both live abroad, a girl and a boy. You can't blame them, Sandra, for not wanting to be bothered with removals.'

'I still think it's disgusting.'

Tamara noticed her mother's anxious glance at Alexandra, quickly converted into the non-judgemental friendliness which is the accepted attitude of a mother towards her adult children. Olga Hoyland had tried to persuade Alexandra to get a part-time help and a part-time job, but Alexandra was committed to the idea that her finest achievement was to give the world her own perfect children, all well-adjusted, clever and healthy as a certain consequence of having been cared for exclusively by their mother. 'Do you really think my time would be better spent as a midwife to other people's sloppy ideas? Editing their sloppy prose? I don't see how you can even suggest it.'

'Not as an alternative, as an extra,' Olga Hoyland had said, but to deaf ears. Yet Olga knew what she was talking about. She was doomed to watch her daughter repeat her own mistakes. She had given up her work at the B.B.C. to look after her own children at a time, in a place, where mothers unquestioningly did so, and like nearly all professionally educated women of her generation, she suffered exactly the same agonies from displacement that would be considered with such serious sympathy in a later era when they were the lot of redundant men. At that time, housewives were expected to thrive on captivity, and it was only when Olga broke out and went back to work that she recognised that she had been a little mad in the preceding years. 'I worried about the stupidest things, like whether I should wash the paintwork once a month or once a week, and whether there should be two or three choices of pudding at our dinner parties.' Once she was sensibly occupied, the paintwork went unwashed and friends came to informal meals, while Olga watched her elder daughter become prey to the same obsessions that she had escaped.

Yet was Tamara in a better state? She could sense her mother's anxieties about her too; so well-qualified and successful in an ideal career, but too thin, too taut, and involved in unspecified extra-curricular activities, about which she never spoke and her parents never asked, whose terrifying traces occasionally showed. Tamara believed that her father had some idea of her secret work for Department E. Passing behind her with a cheese board now, he stroked her yellow hair, and she turned her cheek quickly against his hand before he went on to his own place.

Tamara was usually intrepid, though she feared snakes, and being in huge crowds, but above all those, she dreaded the pain that harm to her would cause her parents. Spies shouldn't have families, she thought savagely, and in fiction few did. Lovers, parents, siblings, children, all were human ties, weakening the trained resolve. Yet without them, would the spy be nothing more than a dangerous machine? Who is to do such work, if not those with something to lose? Qualms may be a necessary limit to ruthlessness.

Alexandra was still talking about her campaign. 'What do you think, Tara? After all, you're in the business of preserving the past. Do you think works of art should be allowed to leave the country? Is it right for some millionaire to have them to gloat over in private?'

'No. They should be available for study.'

'Study. You would say that. It's intellectual snobbery. Why should scholars be more entitled to see them than millionaires? It is ordinary people whose lives need enriching with art.'

'These pictures weren't available for ordinary people before they were sold.'

'That doesn't mean we should perpetuate archaic injustices. Now they have emerged from the prison of private hoarding, they have to stay out in the open. What I . . .' But at this point the baby began to cry and the middle child to whine.

Tamara said to her father, 'Who did own them anyway?'

'He was a client of mine, Captain Leslie, you might remember meeting him occasionally. Nice old chap. But his children have emigrated.'

'How did he come by things like a Gainsborough?'

'Inheritance, I think, and his wife had a lot of her family stuff too, some wonderful furniture as well as the pictures, and the house they lived in. It was a folly, and the Leslies converted it into a house. Mrs Leslie's father inherited it from old Lady Clementine Bessemer, one of the last of a family that once had great estates in Devon. They owned Stockwell, until the middle of the last century I think, but the title went to distant cousins and all Lady Clementine kept was that useless folly – or so she must have thought it – and some unfashionable

121

family portraits. I believe she was quite young at the time, poor girl.'

'How did she support herself?' Olga Hoyland asked.

'She had a post at Court, maid-of-honour to Queen Victoria or something of the kind.'

'An awful way of life,' Olga Hoyland said energetically. 'You remember, girls, hearing Grandmamma talking about it. I should hate it.' Olga's mother had been in attendance on the Czarina, before escaping in 1917. She used to repeat to her family, like folk tales, the saga of her travels through Russia, Mongolia, China, Canada and America. She had experienced more in that year of adventure than most people do in a lifetime.

'I can think of worse fates, at least you would meet some interesting people,' Alexandra said, and Tamara wondered why everything Alexandra said these days sounded like a reproach or a complaint.

'At least it was a roof over her head and a salary,' Rob Hoyland said. 'Clementine Bessemer never married, so she really lived at court. There's a marvellous story of Clem Leslie's father collecting old Lady Clementine's things from Windsor. Lady Clementine herself had died about five years earlier.'

'Tell us the story, Father.'

'Queen Victoria had died in 1901, and left all her personal papers to be sorted out by her youngest child, Princess Beatrice, and she spent the ensuing years casting historical documents onto bonfires in spite of all the protests of the King, the Prince of Wales, and anyone else who had the nerve to remonstrate. She said she had a right to do it and her mamma would have wished it. In those rooms full of the accumulated papers of three quarters of a century, Princess Beatrice came across some packing cases with Lady Clementine Bessemer's name painted on them. She must have stored her personal belongings at Windsor, not having a proper home of her own to put them in. So Princess Beatrice summoned Clem Leslie's father, who was Lady Clementine's great nephew and residuary legatee, to take them away, and she gave him a lecture about preserving them as memorabilia and taking good care of them, and keeping the old lady's memory green, and all the while there she was destroying her own mother's diaries and letters like a madwoman.'

'What did those packing cases have in them?'

'The family portraits, I suppose, among other things. I never heard the details. But that was where Clem Leslie got quite a lot of the antiques she had at the Folly.'

Distrust coincidence, Mr Black had warned, quoting: 'One is a coincidence, two is happenstance, three is enemy action.'

'Can I have a look at the sale catalogue? Is it in the house?' Tamara asked. Although the place looked untidy, the Hoylands could always find what they wanted. The catalogue was in a wooden bowl (carved from one of the dead elm trees removed from their drive) under a roll of half-embroidered canvas and on top of a pile of postcards from the Louvre. The prices were pencilled in beside several of the lots.

'I went along, just for fun,' Olga Hoyland said.

'Fun,' Alexandra muttered jealously.

'I did buy something, that coral teething ring.'

'Was there much jewellery?'

'Nothing very special. Mostly Victorian things like a mourning brooch, full of hair, and lots of jet. It was all sold to Mr Yeo who keeps the antique shop in Stockwell, except for one ring in a separate lot, look, number twenty-nine, intaglio amethyst set in filigree, probably sixteenth century.'

'That's closer to your period, Tara,' Alexandra said.

'Wouldn't you want that kind of thing to be in a public gallery?'

'It ought to be in the British Museum,' Tamara said energetically, and then stopped to laugh at herself. 'You are quite right, Sandra, and I do agree with you. It's just that ancient things get me more worked up. I should like to save treasures for the nation, just like you. Let me make a contribution to your fund.'

After dinner Olga Hoyland offered to put the grand-children to bed, and Alexandra went to talk to Tamara while she unpacked her case.

'It's nice coming home for a visit. I try to bring the children when I can. It doesn't change, does it? Mother runs the place like a machine.'

Tamara drew the familiar chintz curtains across the window, and sniffed at the vase of lily-scented mahonia. 'It isn't so difficult without children around,' she said, trying to console.

Alexandra flung herself onto the bed. 'There always are children around, that's the trouble. Have you got a smoke? I can't when Ben's in the room, or he starts shouting, "Mummy, Mummy, you'll die." It's all that bloody telly, corrupting his mind.'

Tamara unearthed a carton of stale Dunhills from her desk, and watched the nicotine soothe her sister. She said, 'It doesn't seem to work for me.'

'Wish it didn't for me, we can't afford it anyway. Not your problem, that.'

'Not at the moment,' Tamara agreed.

'Not for long, is that it? Is it your bookseller?'

'No.'

'Come on, Tara, who is he? What's his name, what does he do, how long have you known him?'

'I have only just met him, he's an art dealer, he's called Kim.'

124

'Art dealer,' Alexandra muttered.

Tamara added hastily, 'He's the most gorgeous-looking man I have ever seen.'

'Is he more than just a pretty face?' Alexandra had married the prettiest possible face herself.

Tamara said, 'He doesn't look like James, he's more . . . inscrutable. Rugged.'

'I suppose what you mean is that he's marvellous in bed. But is there anything else?'

'You mean getting married and settling down. How would I know? I have not known him long. I don't know much about him, where he comes from, or where he's going, anything. I'm probably being a rash idiot. I know it isn't like me, I'm usually such a one for checking and looking things up and making sure, considering all the alternatives and possibilities.'

'Nonsense, Tara, you are the most impulsive person I know.'

'That's only because I usually reach the same conclusion after thinking things through that I jumped to before. But this time I haven't even tried.'

'He's bewitched you. Have you bewitched him?'

Tamara blushed. 'I don't know.'

'Oh dear. I know it's a good idea to be spontaneous, in theory, I mean, I suppose I would say that,' Alexandra said with a marked lack of spontaneity. 'But, oh Tara, do be careful.'

It was the very next morning that Tamara discovered that she had not been nearly careful enough. Alexandra had driven off after the baby's early feed, to get back to Bristol, in time for the eldest child to go to play group. Tamara came down to have breakfast with her parents before they left for their respective offices.

'What have you got on today, Tamara?'

'One or two bits of fieldwork.'

'Be careful if you go up on the moor. Snow is forecast.'

'One of the places I need to see is at Stockwell.'

'It's not the weather for seeing ancient monuments,' Olga Hoyland said.

'Now that's a coincidence,' Rob Hoyland said. He leafed through the opened letters beside his plate. 'There's a letter here forwarded by the auctioneers who handled the sale at Stockwell Folly for us. Someone who wants to know more about the Leslies: would anyone know where they acquired a particular picture that was in the sale. Funny after what we were saying last night. A Prince Joachim of Horn. What sort of title do you think that is?'

'A German one,' Olga Hoyland said. 'One of my ancestors married into the family. I'll show you.'

A bound volume of her mother's numerous interlocking family trees stood in a bookcase alongside the photograph album, and a copy of the privately printed memoirs of forty years as a county councillor by Rob Hoyland's father.

'Going back a bit of course,' Olga murmured. 'Let's see . . . here we are. It was in eighteen forty. Poor girl, and she died within a year. Childbirth, I suppose.'

Tamara looked where her mother's finger pointed. Sonya, the third of six children, born 1826, died 1844, married in 1843 to Siegfried Frederick, second son of the reigning Prince of Horn und Reiss und Drachensfeld.

'Joachim von Horn und Reiss und Drachensfeld,' Rob Hoyland rolled the name on his tongue.

Joachim von Reiss. Chim Reiss. Kim Rice, Tamara thought. She felt her skin burning and a chill in her stomach. Her heart was beating very fast and sweat started out on her forhead, the physical signs of realising that one has made a disastrous mistake.

126

XVII

Tamara waited to ring Department E until her parents had left the house. She sat pretending to concentrate on the *Western Morning News*, which carried an article about the forthcoming exhibition of treasures from East Germany, and discussing the softening of political attitudes that this initiative represented.

James Bond had fallen for the charms of girls who turned out to be working for his enemies. George Smiley's wife let him down over and over again. There was no reason to expect secret agents to be less foolish about the opposite sex than anyone else. But that was no comfort. My famous bloody intuition, Tamara thought.

'Will you be in for dinner tonight, Tamara?' her mother asked.

Kim had not actually lied to her. Perhaps he always used the democratic name. Why should he tell a casual girl friend who he really was, or about his interest in his family's treasure? Tamara had not told him anything about herself.

'Come and have lunch with me if you are anywhere near the office,' her father said.

It was not his reticence, it was what she knew from Mr Black that was burning a brand in Tamara's self-esteem. A neo-Nazi, a fanatical right-wing Catholic revivalist. That was what Joachim von Horn und Reiss und

Drachensfeld was – that, and a pretty face.

If it had been only his pretty face I fell for, she thought, it would have been all right.

'See you tonight,' Olga Hoyland called, slamming the front door.

Am I so desperate to find a man that I don't see what the ones I fancy are really like? she asked herself dismally. Am I so indifferent to the responsibilities I chose to take on? Should I have known that with Kim Rice I was mixing up business and pleasure?

Intellectual honesty required the answer, 'yes'.

Mrs Uglow said that Mr Black was in a meeting. She always told callers that.

'But Mrs Uglow, it's me, Tamara Hoyland.'

'I am very sorry, Dr Hoyland, but he really is at a meeting this time. He's not even in the building.'

'Do you expect him back soon?'

'Not today at all.'

Not that it made much difference. What could he have said that Tamara did not already say, more viciously, to herself? Would he have summoned her straight back to London, or told her to get on with it, using her emotional impulses instead of being used by them.

Another call, after a tiresome session with Directory Enquiries; the young art dealer. Had he been the one to offer the Italian painting to Kim Rice? 'No, no, of course not, I'd never heard of him. He rang me up and said he'd heard that I'd got a primitive and could he have a look? Why do you ask? I hope there isn't anything . . .'

Tamara assured him that he could count on the sale going ahead. And may I be forgiven, she thought, certain that Kim Rice would never go near the young man again. Having got his excuse for going hunting on Artemis's home ground, where would he begin? Presumably in exactly the same place as Tamara proposed to search.

Microdots of snow were beginning to fall on the higher ground as Tamara drove towards the moor, and once over the top, the Folly at Stockwell appeared suddenly as the road descended from a high curve. It was a castellated tower, with windows like arrow slits and a nail-studded front door. In the North it would have been a Peel Tower. Here it was exactly what it was called, a folly, which had been designed to decorate the view for the inhabitants of the Big House.

Monuments from the more distant past, for whose remains Tamara had a professional responsibility, were scattered over the landscape. Within the circle of her vision were two clusters of hut circles, a standing stone, and a memorial to men fallen in the Napoleonic wars. The moors stretched away, bare, brown, speckled with white where last week's snow still lay on the north facing slopes. A line as neat as geometry divided the empty land from the wet, midwinter-green fields.

On the south side of the tower was desolation.

The original quarrying must have started behind a hill and out of sight. Perhaps the machinery and explosives had spoken of prosperity, employment, dividends for the landowners, a prudent use of the earth's bounty. The Bessemers probably congratulated themselves that they were sitting on a fortune.

Now, immediately below the tower, was a huge, rough heap of spoil glistening from afar, and even admirable to those who saw the tower as part of a wide sweep of country, but from close by greyish brown, speckled and tabby, only gleaming bright where the snow still lay on it. The excavations for china clay had crept towards the tower, consuming the hill, the hollows, gouging out great holes in the ground and leaving behind them, when all the valuable material had gone, the foretaste of an icy hell, where nothing could grow, all dirty, and useless. Even the water that filled the deeper pits was a wicked green, the kind of colour used by pharmacists to warn that a liquid would be poisonous.

The tower was empty. Soon it would be gone, literally as though it had never been, leaving no trace for the field worker to detect, for the very ground on which it stood would disappear, its elements reconstituted into utensils, cosmetics, or the glaze on paper, and no reminders would stay in the useless spoil to denote a house in which a family had lived for as long, at least, as anyone now living could remember.

The house, abandoned and due to be demolished, had of course been vandalised. Tamara entered through one of several broken windows, and found the detritus of irresponsible occupation lay in every room. But the kitchen and bathrooms contained modern fitments, central heating pipes followed the skirting boards, and there was recent electrical wiring. It must have been a comfortable home. The big house, Stockwell itself, stood in a derelict park about half a mile away, its long façade visible from this angle with a full complement of chimneys, columns, porticoes, and blind-looking windows. The new road to the china-clay workings, which Tamara had come on, had cut across the parkland, separating the tower from the house, so that one could no longer see the path that must have once led strollers towards this pretty peep. The actual drive to the house turned off what might have been an earlier highway, further down the hillside. Even from this distance, it could be seen that the drive was rutted and unrepaired, and that it led to an area of overgrown ground in front of the house. A red car was parked on it.

The uneven surface of the drive scraped on the bottom

of Tamara's tiny car, though it could have done no harm to Kim's well-sprung Saab. Tamara parked beside it, making no attempt at quietness, but he did not appear. The wide steps were cracked and crumbling, and there seemed to be no bell or knocker. There must be a back door.

Tamara walked along the frontage of the house. The windows were set too high above the ground for her to see into them, and the area windows were shuttered. There should once have been a footpath running along the side wall, but now undisciplined vegetation came right up to it. Tamara picked her way through it.

She was perfectly used to visiting lonely monuments; it was part of her job. Why then, she wondered, did Stockwell seem so frighteningly deserted? Was it the unformulated thought of ghosts, or traps, or 'nasty men' that made her tread so softly, peer so carefully ahead, listen so anxiously for non-existent sounds?

The side of the house was almost as long as its front. On round the corner, then, and on to – nothing. There was no back wall. Where the rear of the house should be was open space.

The façade and most of the two side walls of Stockwell were propped upright by immense wooden scaffolds. The back wall had disappeared completely, probably in the fire that had left blackened patches all over the interior walls, grotesquely alternated with patterned paper and plasterwork. Somebody had repainted the outside of the remaining walls since the fire. Where the ground floor rooms had been, thistles and docks were growing.

There must once have been pleasant lawns at the back of this now desolate house, planted with specimen trees, fragrant with box hedges and flowers, sloping gently to a stream. It was all grazing land now, with the odd tree still standing. Another folly had been erected where the stream broadened into a small lake. There was a stone bridge, Chinese-style, curving over the water, and a pathway to a tiny temple with a greenish roof.

The little monument consisted of a circle of pillars around a marble statue, about three-quarters life size, of a goddess, naked except for some tactful draperies, poised on one foot with the other raised behind her. In one hand she held a small bow, on her back a quiver of arrows: Diana, the huntress, or Artemis. Tamara recalled the words Artemis von Horn had written: *In the shared care of the huntress and her sister.*

Kim Rice, the Prince of Horn, emerged from the shadow of the domed roof. Tamara drew back behind a broken wall and watched him through her powerful miniature binoculars.

The statue stood on a pedestal made of stone, with bronze plates inset on its four sides. Kim bent to a bag that was lying on the steps and took out a rolled toolkit. With one instrument he poked at the rivets that fastened the plates to the plinth, then he took a different tool, with a larger blade, and began to probe the cracks between the metal and the stone. Two of the plaques fitted too tightly for the wedge to enter; the third allowed him to ease it in, deeper and deeper, until he was able to take a hammer and go round the outline of the metal with gentle taps on the implement's handle, and lift the bronze plate away. He set it on the ground, and took a torch from his toolkit.

Tamara replaced the binoculars in her bag, and walked across the pasture towards him. He was kneeling, peering into the cavity. He took a couple of things out of it without much care, and put them on the ground behind him, a china doll, and a yellow box. When Tamara was close enough she saw that it was made of bone, with a picture of the Great Exhibition of 1851 incised on it.

'Hello, Kim,' she said.

Kim Rice stood up and whirled round in a smooth movement.

'Did you follow me here?'

'Follow you, Kim? Of course not. But aren't you pleased to see me?' She stepped closer to him, wetting her lips, reaching for him. He was wearing a blue padded anorak, and his teeth gleamed against his pale brown skin. He looks like a ski instructor, she thought – desirable, available, and faithless.

He embraced her ardently. She thought, he doesn't trust me either.

'What are you doing here, Tamara?'

'My job. I told you that I work for the Royal Commission on Historical Monuments.'

'Is this one of your monuments?'

'Of course. It's very important. Stockwell is an excellent example of its period. And these follies, of course, we are always anxious to preserve.'

'What a pity for me. I was hoping to buy this statue,' he said plausibly. 'That's why I am examining it so closely.'

'Is that what you came here for, Kim?'

'No, it's a diversion. I came down to see if I could trace the history of the picture you saw with me. It came from that peculiar looking place you can see on the skyline. I hoped that if I asked around a bit ... But I was distracted by this. Do you think I might be able to get the whole temple dismantled?'

'That might not be easy. Have you found anything in there?'

'It seems to have been a kids' hiding place. Nothing but toys.'

'May I look?'

133

She took his torch, and crouched to peer inside the dark cavity. As he had said, it was a child's hiding place. Still inside remained some dolls' teacups and a pile of varied shells. Kim had already pocketed, with a swift movement that Tamara might well not have seen, a small oilcloth packet. There was no treasure.

Now that Kim was standing under the shadow of the roof, Tamara could not see his face, only a dim blur, and the powerful shape of his body.

This was what she had seen that day last week, when she had gone into Margot Ellice's room and found her struggling with a tall man whose face was concealed behind a stocking-mask.

Kim held out his hand for the torch. There was still a bandage on his wrist, from the wound Tamara had inflicted on him that day.

Was he looking for the treasure, having learnt from Margot Ellice's research that it might exist still in England? Had he stolen the papers, or destroyed them, to make sure that nobody else would have that knowledge? Where would I look now, if I were Kim, Tamara wondered, twining herself closely to him, accepting his caresses. For a moment she feared that her treacherous body would respond; but all her delight was simulated. She moved her hands artfully under his jacket. He turned up at Jeremy Ellice's that evening, she thought, to trace Margot; Grandpapa's ladylike housekeeper must have told him where her predecessor was – or the hospital, perhaps. And he went back the next day. He killed Margot and destroyed the papers. But why did he ask me to meet him again?

They drew a little apart. 'It's so cold here. Let's go back to the cars.' They walked closely together.

He saw that I had read Margot's manuscript, Tamara thought. He wanted to find out whether I knew any more than there was in the first part of it.

He held his arm around her shoulders, walking close at her side. 'I thought I'd try to find any old friends of the people who owned that picture,' he said. 'Somebody might still know where they got it.'

'That's a good idea.'

'But I didn't have any luck. Nobody knows anything. So I'm going back to London. We shall look forward to being in your flat together again, mmm?' Standing beside his car, they kissed like Hollywood film stars. When Tamara opened her eyes, she saw that his were wandering. She redoubled her efforts. When she got into her own car, and followed the red one that Kim had hired down the drive, the oilskin packet he had found in the care of Artemis Bessemer's divine namesake was in her own pocket. Kim winked his headlights and turned southwards across the moor. Tamara tooted on her horn, and turned towards the nearest village.

Tamara had been taught to pick pockets by an Egyptian, at her postgraduate seminary in London. He told his class that he had been able to whisk wallets from pockets before he could speak. It had been an amusing lesson. Strong men, who delighted in shooting and hand-to-hand combat, grew fumble fingered and embarrassed when instructed to go out into the streets and return with three credit cards. They did not think it quite nice, unlike learning to kill and wound. Tamara was the star pupil. She brought Sayid the trophy of an invitation card for an investiture at Buckingham Palace, but insisted on returning it, anonymously, by post. Sayid was very disappointed. He had hoped to use it himself.

Tamara parked in a lay-by to examine this haul. She unfastened the twine that was wrapped around the oilcloth, and peeled back the layers of waterproof covering. Safer than Clementine's trunks at Windsor,

135

safer than her own little house with Philip Lambert, Artemis would have thought her childhood hiding place. She had used it for the legal proof of her son's rights. There were two sheets of stiff paper: the certificate of her marriage with Joachim von Horn, and the birth certificate of their son, written in the old fashioned German Gothic script. Tamara made out Artemis's name, and Joachim's, and that of Heinrich Joachim Sigismund Bolko Frederick.

There was no way of knowing whether Philip Lambert ever told Henry who he really was and to what his mother had believed he was entitled. Here, untouched since he was a small child, was the evidence of his claim. It could surely represent no threat to the present Prince of Horn. But Tamara slotted the certificates carefully between the pages of her road map of the British Isles, and replaced the book in the side pocket of her car.

XVIII

During their childhood at Stockwell, Artemis and Clementine Bessemer would seldom have entered the village and never have been allowed inside any of the houses, except perhaps the parsonage. It was a 'Rest Home for Pensioners' now.

Two of the shops in the village were closed for the winter, one a Craft Centre, the other a Gift and Souvenir Shoppe. Between them and the General Store stood a small thatched chapel and a row of old cottages which would have been pitiful cob hovels in Artemis's day, now all very spruce and painted in rainbow colours. The grey tower of the Church poked up between the stripped branches of a clump of dead elm trees.

Indira Patel, Licensed to Sell Wine and Spirits, was not a descendant of the hovel dwellers. She wore a sari, had a red spot between her eyebrows, and spoke with a Midlands accent. She was knitting something lacy in pale blue wool, and apologised for it.

'It's the Saturday Market in the town, you see, I want to get it finished in time.' There was a poster advertising a Bring and Buy Stall in aid of the Peace Movement; others invited people to an Any Questions evening in the village hall, a Paper Mountain in the car park, a Jumble Sale at the Primary School, a Coffee Morning at 'Tor View, by kind permission of Mr and Mrs Carwardine', and a performance of *Pygmalion* at the Comprehensive School.

Mrs Patel knew exactly who would be able to tell Tamara about the Leslies. 'You're the second person to ask me that today. Gorgeous he was. An artist, I think, something to do with a painting. Anyway, Miss Christie will know everything. Friends from way back, she and Mrs Leslie were.' She gave directions for finding Miss Christie's house at Stockcross as though she had lived in the area all her life. Tamara bought some fruit, and as she was paying for it Jeremy Ellice, more shabby and shaggy than ever, hunched into a sheepskin coat worn shiny and patched with dirt, came into the shop.

He said to Tamara, 'I saw your car outside. I have to talk to you. I was so upset – I mean, here you are, not expecting any trouble, planning your article for *Antiquity* – I feel responsible.'

'Let's get out of Mrs Patel's way, shall we?' It was snowing properly now, though it melted as it fell and a fierce wind numbed human nerves.

'Sorry, it's just I was so glad to find you. The thing is this, Tamara, I saw the policeman in charge of Margot's case and it looks as though – it seems hardly credible – but they seem to think it wasn't an accident. They actually think she might have been murdered!'

Tamara mimed astonishment.

'Yes, they say that she was unconscious before the fire. They think that she was left there to breathe in the fumes on purpose. The pathologist . . .'

'That's horrid news for you, Jeremy, I am sorry. But why did it make you follow me all the way down here?'

'It suddenly occurred to me that the only thing it could possibly have to do with was the treasure, and I thought of you looking round down here – I was worried. If whoever did it thought that Margot was the only one

138

who knew anything about it, and then found out that you were on the trail too, you might be in danger yourself. Well, I couldn't . . . I mean to say, I know how capable you are, but it wouldn't . . .'

'How sweet of you to worry about me.'

'I tried to ring your flat but there was no answer. And then I guessed . . . it only took me three hours to get here. Such a relief to see your little car here.'

'Get in, won't you? It's so cold.' If Kim saw her here with Jeremy Ellice it would remove any lingering doubts he might have about her part in this affair.

'Yes, and then you can look at this letter. It was forwarded from your grandfather's flat.'

The envelope, addressed to Ms Margot Ellice, was superscribed 'The University of Buriton'. The letter inside, from the head of the department of Modern History, Professor Dwerryhouse, began with the usual apologetic incantation about the delay in replying to Miss Ellice's query.

However, I was glad to have the incentive to refresh my own memory about Philip Lambert, since he is a minor figure of some importance in the philosophical thought of the last century, and is of especial interest to me, as I am at present working on the allied subject of the French political thinkers of the second half of that era. As you rightly point out, little is known of Lambert's personal life. The entry in the Dictionary of National Biography is brief indeed, and describes only his academic work. There are, however, one or two references to him in the published letters and memoirs of the period, from which I deduce that he was not a native-born Englishman, though I can find no evidence to suggest that he was a political refugee, nor any pointer to his country of origin. His works, as you know, are published in the English language, and in French. I think it likely that he was a member of that circle of political emigrés like Karl Marx himself, who settled in London, and I should perhaps suggest to you that it would be worth trying to find out whether there is some record of his having been a regular reader at the British Museum.

I have mentioned your query to my colleague, Dr Jacob, who is currently writing a history of Palestine in the pre-Mandate period. He tells me that he believes your Philip Lambert to be one of the Jewish philanthropists who collected money in Europe to purchase land in Palestine upon which impoverished Zionists might settle. In that case, since there may have been some association with the Baron de Rothschild, you might find the Rothschild archives a fruitful source of information. No doubt you have access to the various libraries specialising in Jewish affairs. I assume that you are also aware that Lambert's published work shows him to have been an anti-monarchist egalitarian. You may not have come across an article published in the (rather obscure) Journal of Equality, *of which only three issues appeared, in 1893 to 4. I enclose a photocopy of Lambert's proposals for a political system without titles or honours, which still reads very well today. Do let me know if there is anything else I can tell you, and meanwhile I wish you all success with your researches into this fascinating period . . .*

'How properly Margot was going about this work,' Tamara said.

'She had a teach-yourself book called *How to do Research*, I got in a sale somewhere.'

'Good heavens,' Tamara said faintly; it was a depressing but poignant thought.

'What about your own research?' Jeremy asked. 'I take it you have been asking around about the treasure. When I heard you had come down here I guessed it must be what you were doing.'

Tamara found that Jeremy, weedy and incompetent as he looked, was impossible to dislodge. In the end she mentally shrugged her shoulders and took him with her to call upon Miss Christie.

'I have lived here for nearly half a century you know,' Miss Christie said. 'Worked here, made a life here, though they still think of me as an incomer. But when you asked me about Clemmie Leslie it's the old days that come to mind. The very old days, many years ago, not recent times at all. No, I have such a clear picture of the time before the war, when I first came here. I moved to Devon to be near to Clem; we had been friends since our Somerville days.'

Miss Christie was thin and busy. She went on with her work as she spoke, cutting shapes of cream coloured silk out of a bale of fabric, at a large polished table. She was making smocked nightdresses. 'I am setting up a mail-order business, I expect a very steady turnover; women want handmade goods in natural materials. It is so important to keep busy once one has retired, and I've always believed in the value of handwork. I used to encourage my girls to make things; it was always difficult to make time in the curriculum, but it's so important to combine academic and practical skills. I am afraid that we haven't struck the right balance in modern education. When society begins to value the carpenter as highly as the banker . . . have you acquired manual skills, my dear?'

'I am quite handy, yes. Archaeologists usually know how things ought to work, even if they can't make them.'

Miss Christie nodded. 'A very good training. I shall use it as an example in my next speech.'

Miss Christie had been the headmistress of a private girls' school which had closed down very recently. 'But I really admire what they are doing at our local comprehensive school,' she said, her scissors twinkling in the beam of her spot light. 'They have made me a governor now. Of course, my own working life was spent in much easier circumstances, our girls were preselected for their will to co-operate. But once Clem had gone . . .'

'Mrs Leslie was a teacher too?'

'Yes, we always worked together. History was her subject. She used to help out part-time until the children were out of the way. And that took years as there was twelve years between them. Artemis wasn't born until after Will Leslie came back in 1944.'

'They live abroad, don't they?'

'Nigel runs a hotel in California, and Artemis went to a kibbutz in Israel. The young do such unexpected things. Clem would as soon have expected her daughter to become the Pope of Rome, as an orthodox Jew.'

'Was Mrs Leslie a Roman Catholic?'

'No, no, she was an atheist, but her background was Jewish. Not practising, that's why Artemis surprised us so much.'

Tamara explained that it was Clem Leslie's background about which she hoped to learn. 'It's because I'm trying to trace the history of one of their pictures.'

'The Gainsborough, I suppose. It's a Bessemer, of course. You knew that my friend Clem inherited the Folly, as well as her pictures, from her father, who had it from an old aunt called Lady Clementine Bessemer. None of that family left here now, alas.' Miss Christie arranged her paper patterns onto another stretch of silk. 'Just hand me that pin cushion, would you my dear? Yes, I knew Clem Lambert's family – that was her maiden name – better than my own in some ways. I am afraid I outgrew my relations, they never could understand what made me want to go to college; all they wanted for me was to marry and have children and a comfortable home. Now the Lamberts, they were quite unconventional. They'd spent a good deal of time in Palestine, as it was called then, they were involved in

142

purchasing land from the Turks for Jewish emigrés to live in, and collecting funds for them. Of course, by the time I met him old Henry Lambert was too old for the travelling any more, he'd settled down in London, but he often spoke about his work there, it was always so interesting. His son, that was Clem's father, was killed in the first war. So many boys died in that war.' Miss Christie's voice remained steady, but her shears swerved into the material, and, tutting, she put them to one side and tore off the length of ruined cloth. 'I really must concentrate, it's such a waste otherwise. In any case, I am sure you didn't want to hear all that. It's the Bessemers you will have to study, to trace the pictures. They were all old Lady Clementine's.'

Miss Christie cleared the table of silk and laid it with tea and scones. Tamara sustained a conversation about her own education, career and background. She said:

'We used to play your school at games.'

'I didn't realise you were one of the Devon Hoylands,' Miss Christie said. 'I remember your grandfather when he was the Chairman of the Education Committee.'

Tamara suddenly remembered Miss Christie too. 'You were the judge in the Drama Competition! You told me I'd mangled the metre in *To be or not to be*.'

'Were you Hamlet?' Jeremy Ellice exclaimed.

Miss Christie nodded briskly. 'One of the benefits of single sex education.'

'It certainly meant I got some decent parts,' Tamara said. 'Otherwise I'd have been made to play the *ingénue* every time.'

'That's exactly what I told them when those competitions began.' Miss Christie pushed back her chair, taking her weight on her wrists to rise. 'I still have the programmes somewhere. You would have disapproved,

143

Mr Ellice. Girls fighting, fencing, and swaggering around in black tights and sword belts.' Ignoring his disclaimer, she brought a box file over to the table. Tamara joined her in leafing through a stack of fading sheets of duplicator paper, arranged in chronological order, and going back over many years. Almost at once, Tamara found the play bills showing her own name, and felt a curious nostalgia for days that she would hate to re-live. She showed them to Jeremy: Tamara Hoyland as Hamlet, as Macbeth, as Portia and Rosalind. On another page, where Alexandra's name was shown as the 'First Messenger', Titania was played by Artemis Leslie.

'I remember it!' Tamara said. 'I had been taken to see my sister, I can't have been more than five or six, but I can still remember the Queen kissing the donkey. She had the most beautiful hair, apricot coloured.'

'All my girls played some part. I thought being on the stage so good for them, it gives confidence, and they learnt to speak up and stand up. We had big perform-ances every term. One of the parents built a proper stage for the assembly hall, and after a few years we had gathered as good a wardrobe as most small theatres can supply. The girls used to bring things from their homes, and sometimes we would get donations from shops. One girl brought in her grandfather's uniform, he'd been in the Brigade of Guards, and another found a cupboard full of eighteenth-century dresses. Nobody would pay money for second-hand clothes in those days, though now some of them would be regarded as museum pieces I expect.'

'Did Mrs Leslie provide things? There must have been quite a lot in the Folly.'

'Yes, we had a whole trunkful from Clem. It had belonged to her great grandmother, the one she named Artemis after. It had never been opened, just stored

144

away by Lady Clementine somewhere, until it came down here along with the other things that were inherited from her. That was after the Lamberts' house in London was sold, and Clem and Will Leslie decided to convert the Folly. We believed in The Countryside in those days, it was the fashion – back to the soil, and the dignity of physical labour, and the degradation of towns. But of course Will was seldom here to till the soil, he was away in the navy, which is one of the reasons Clem was glad to have mè nearby.'

'So you acquired a lot of the Victorian things that had belonged to Lady Artemis Bessemer?'

Miss Christie looked surprised at being dragged back to that subject, but answered readily enough. 'It was the sort of collection nobody can face sorting out. Old clothes, and brushes with hairs straggling through the bristles, and a good deal of that heavy Victorian jewellery our Victorian ancestors liked, glass, and beads, nothing valuable and all perfectly hideous. It was just the wrong time to have unpacked that trunk; if we had left it longer the clothes would have seemed charming, but to us they were disgustingly dowdy. Clem insisted that I should choose something to keep so I took a ridiculously ornate vase. Terribly tasteless and Victorian, pinchbeck, with ugly purple and green glass ornaments on it. I used to use it for hyacinths. Of course, the Victorians liked loud colours. I remember my own mother in magenta and maroon and yellow ochre.'

'I should love to see it,' Tamara said.

Miss Christie looked surprised. 'Really? I am afraid I haven't got it any more. I gave it to Mrs Patel for the Peace Movement's stall. A real white elephant, I'm afraid. I told her she wouldn't get much for it, but she seemed quite pleased, nice woman that she is.'

145

There were deep blue hyacinths on the window ledges, planted in plastic pots of Wedgwood design, and a china basin with blue roses on it.

'Look,' Miss Christie pointed to the basin. 'That was Artemis's too, but that's charming, I would hate to lose that. Copeland, I believe.'

The heavy scent made Tamara's head swim.

Jeremy said, 'I don't suppose that a flower pot would have been much use to your drama wardrobe.'

'No, that's why I chose it, there were other more attractive things; I should have liked a crucifix, for instance, just glass, nothing valuable, but rather handsome I thought. But that was the year we were doing Henry the Eighth; it was just right for Cardinal Wolsey. And of course the whole trunk was full of useful things. Some of them most unexpected, I must say, and we found some very useful props – a sword, for instance. Nigel insisted on keeping that of course, but we got it when he was grown too old for dressing up. Yes, we were extremely well provided, in that department.'

The regalia of Charles the Great used to adorn amateur dramatics; Tamara wondered whether it was tragic or laughable.

'Miss Christie, what happened to everything in your school, after it closed down?'

'We sold the buildings, of course. I say we, I mean the trustees. It was bought by the West Devon Health Authority to be a geriatric hospital, so I may yet end my days under the same roof.'

'And the equipment?'

'Why do you ask? No – don't tell me, I am sure you have your reasons. It's been my lifelong principle to answer reasonable questions from the young. Always remember when you are dealing with children how important it is not to stunt their natural curiosity. The

146

mind must be allowed freedom to expand and grow.'

'The equipment . . . ?'

'Let me see. We sold some of it by tender. I was quite surprised at the demand for good solid desks and tables, even those as old as mine. The fashion seems to be changing from spindly metal legs that trip you up and nasty laminated surfaces. The boys' school over in Carmell took a good deal of the furniture. I could check if you are really interested.'

'What about everything else?'

'I simply passed it on to the new comprehensive. After all, in a way it's the successor to my school. I wish them well. I rather think that the days of private education are over, though you won't want to hear about that, my dear. Well, all schools need extra equipment, new costumes, props, that sort of thing, if they are to have a high standard for drama. I believe that they were genuinely grateful.'

XIX

I cannot tell how I tell, she thought, but it's certain that I depend on such certainties. Tamara shook her head, and willed herself to concentrate. This was no time for being diverted by the ambiguities of the English language. It was unnecessary to identify the source of her knowledge that she had been followed, and that danger waited. What mattered was to realise it.

Kim Rice? Jeremy Ellice?

Which of them was waiting there in the car park?

Tamara had gone straight to the school after parting from Jeremy Ellice. It was a sprawling expanse of glass and imported brick, its three storeys towering incongruously in a landscape of small fields and stone cottages. Rows of buses waited beside the teachers' cars in the car park, for the two thousand children came from villages as far as fifteen miles away. The bell was ringing just as Tamara approached, and she waited, parked in a row of mothers, while the buses filled and the car park emptied. She kept hairpins and cosmetics in the glove compartment, and used them now to conventionalise her appearance, removing an Italian knitted coat of many colours to stand up in navy blue anonymity suitable for a teacher.

Heat and the invariable smell of schools were bottled up inside the glass entrance hall, parquet floored, littered and lined with notices that flapped on their pins in the hot air arising from the radiators below them. A boy and girl, kissing as they walked, went by without a sideways glance. An elderly man hustled out muttering like the White Rabbit; two middle-aged men, complaining loudly about the fourth year, left the building with their piles of exercise books.

At the back of the hall a long wide corridor led past rows of darkened classrooms. Tamara entered one to find a stack of notebooks, which she carried in the crook of her arm like a badge of pedagogic office, and went back to the hall. She stood at a slight angle to a notice board that was covered with invitations to sign on for educational trips to European capital cities, and tried to decipher the direction boards without obviously staring at them.

A young man in denim and sandals said, 'You observe that young Crosthwaite signed on for the Aegean cruise, having been let off his fine for under-age drinking because the family pleaded poverty.'

'So he has,' Tamara said. 'Isn't that just typical.'

'You on your way in or out?'

'In.'

'You shouldn't do it, you know, it's overtime,' he said, carrying on towards the outer door.

The signs were painted on white arrows of wood clustered round a central post. Tamara could see the way to the administrative offices, headmaster's room, deputy headmaster's room, assistant deputy headmistress's room and secretary. She crossed the hall, and stood beside the Head Boy's notice board. He, like the Assistant Head Girl, was full of worthy exhortations to his flock.

For a moment Tamara allowed her thoughts to wander resentfully in the by-ways of feminism. She watched a woman, with a shopping basket over her arm,

149

and a pile of the inevitable exercise books slipping from her grasp, run from the building. *Girls from the fifth year domestic science group will provide the refreshments*, the Head Boy promised those who came to discuss nuclear disarmament; the board next door invited actors to audition for next term's play, *Henry IV Part I*. Tamara had once played the part of Hotspur. Not much chance for the girls of this establishment to indulge in the glorious showing-off of the stage duel, dying gallantly on a half breath, no – 'Percy, thou art dust and food for . . .'. Miss Christie had been right about that.

From this angle the sign showing the way to the auditorium was visible. Tamara walked down empty passages, down steps, up steps, through a gymnasium where enthusiasts were playing badminton, past a row of rooms full of cookers, sewing machines and ironing boards, and eventually to a double door labelled 'Auditorium'.

Tamara pushed it a little open, to hear a voice declaiming: 'I find that the moment I let a woman make friends with me she becomes jealous, exacting, suspicious and a damned nuisance.' Professor Higgins with a Devon accent.

A smaller door led into a passage that skirted the auditorium. Tamara marched along it into another lobby where some girls and boys were waiting with their copies of *Pygmalion*, some muttering their lines, others pushing and giggling like any children told to keep quiet. The voices of the actors came through from the stage; Eliza Doolittle spoke country not cockney.

Tamara whispered to a studious girl, 'Where's the wardrobe?'

'There's nobody there now, Miss. Mrs Davey had to get into the shops before closing time.'

'That doesn't matter, thanks. I just have to . . .'

The girl pointed at another unlit passage. Tamara nodded her thanks. A self confident air will get you everywhere, she told herself, and carried on into the wardrobe room. She shut the door and pulled the blind down before turning on the light to reveal racks of period costumes, shelves of head-dresses, stacks of props. It was well equipped indeed, but, luckily, logically arranged. Tamara was quickly able to narrow down her search to a stack of drawers containing 'knights in armour' props.

Most of the swords were plastic. One, its broken blade rusty, with lumps of stone — or of what could be taken for glass — on the pommel, was heavy: a real weapon.

And the crown? There was a deep drawer stuffed with gilt coronets with mothy velvet centres, with cardboard bent into a circle and sprayed with gold paint, with glitters of fake tiaras. One studded headdress looked likely, but when Tamara pulled it from the drawer it weighed no heavier than a straw hat.

A smaller cabinet contained jewellery, ropes of pearls, flamboyant rings, glass set into pendants. One drawer was full of dandyish shoe or belt buckles. In it there were six segments of metal, folded together, each blackened by age so that no shimmer of silver remained. The plaques were decorated with chunks of stone, and attached together by tiny hooks, so that when they were held upright and shaped into a curve they formed a circlet.

The cross had become detached. Tamara found it in a polythene bag, along with a wooden pectoral cross of the type worn by bishops and cardinals, and the top curve of a carved crozier.

It had been used by generations of children; it had lain unidentified for years. Tamara held the crown and sword, waiting for the flash of emotion that would indicate a portent, or some warning of sacrilege. She could induce no mystic certainty in herself. But her

151

trained intellect and experience in identifying objects from the distant past were an adequate substitute for logic-less vibrations. Here, used to confer mimic royalty on amateur actors in a modern school, were the crown and sword of Charlemagne.

Tamara chose a canvas bag from a peg on the wall, and wrapped her trophies in a Bedouin shawl before putting them into it. She turned off the light and raised the blind. It was then, in the beam of a departing teacher's headlights, that she saw the brief movement, obscured by the falling snow, of someone lurking beside her own parked car.

The window opened smoothly, and no watcher could see it on this dark face of the building. Snow came settling softly and quickly onto the window sill, like Christmas cotton wool. There were flower beds full of hardy shrubs against the school walls. Tamara dropped the canvas bag onto the ground between the wall and a clump of evergreen laurel, and even as she looked where it had fallen, concealing snow began to cover it. She shut the window and screwed the catch tight before returning through the now empty passages to the front of the building.

A young man in a track suit was leaving too. Tamara smiled and chatted enticingly to him so that he walked beside her to her car and stayed close, leaning on the roof. Tamara waved her empty hands, and managed to spill the contents of her shoulder bag onto the ground. She and the young man picked them up together. She pulled her belt tight over her narrow coat: look, no treasure.

The young man held her door open, and went on talking until she had started the engine and begun to move away.

No persistent headlights followed her home.

*

October 1st, 1863

Your Serene Highness should know that the widow of Prince Joachim von Horn, formerly the Lady Artemis Bessemer, died after a long illness on September 3rd. She had long since ceased to wish that her son should return to his father's country or inherit his worldly dignities. He will be educated by the man whom he knows as his father, and live ignorant of a name, Heinrich von Horn, that your Serene Highness may safely forget, and of the fortune and status that pertain to it. He will be known to himself and the world as the son of one whose name is no longer Ehrenstamm.

That name, Tamara thought, would mean nothing to Nigel Leslie, had meant nothing to her father, nor would either of them know more about its recipient than that he must have been the then reigning Prince of Horn. The copy, or draft, of the letter had been in old Captain Leslie's papers, and Rob Hoyland was sending it on. *Although you and Artemis told me to forward nothing to you, I am sure that this paper, which came to light when I was clearing up your father's orderly affairs, should be disposed of by you in person, especially as it may mean something to you. I have had a translation made from the German, which is attached. If you wish, I can have enquiries set in train to elucidate the matter.*

Pompous language that even that most umpompous of lawyers, her father, used when dictating letters to their clients, Tamara thought. She shuffled the letters back into the pile on her father's desk, and replaced what she had taken from the revolving stand that held Rob Hoyland's reference books; he often brought his work home.

Lawyers needn't know the law, he'd sometimes said, just where to look it up. Tamara was no lawyer, but she had spent three vacations earning money in her father's office, and her prolonged education had taught her, if nothing else, where and how to look almost anything up.

153

There seemed to be no doubt that the regalia she had found would be the subject of litigation from now till Kingdom Come; what with the complications of private international law, of the recognition of states, of the disposal of enemy property, the acquisition of title to stolen property, the loss of title by passage of time, the ownership of princely paraphernalia, the existence of a substitute, previously unrecognised as such, for that paraphernalia – the list would delight those who set law exams, and give an examinee heart failure. As for the political complications – Tamara could not force her tired mind to think of them. It was unlike her to sleep badly, though perhaps this was the right house for insomnia to strike if it had to, for the sitting room was warm all night with big logs smouldering in the wood burning stove, there was plenty to read, and no likelihood of disturbing her sleeping parents whose room was above the kitchen.

But Tamara found it impossible to settle down with any of the books she found. She had made herself a hot drink, stood watching the falling snow out of the window, done some energetic exercises, read the invitation cards on the mantelpiece and the papers on the desk – and felt more wide awake than ever.

What must Waldemar von Horn have felt when he received that communication from the untraceable Philip Ehrenstamm? Relieved that no rival to his title would turn up in later life? Angry that the treasure seemed to be gone for good? He had announced the death of Artemis and her son, whose disappearance must have been kept from the outside world during the intervening two years; half a century later he had employed a jeweller to make a copy of the treasure for his vault. Ironically, the jeweller used the sketches whose publication had so annoyed Prince Waldemar, as the best representation of what he was to copy.

XX

'The satellite picture's useful when it's snowing,' Olga Hoyland said.

'You don't have to apologise for watching your own television.'

'Somehow one feels one has to in the morning.'

The west country was said to be cut off by snow; drifts blocked the main railway lines and roads.

'Cut off from where, I should like to know?' Rob Hoyland asked. The satellite picture showed a broad band of white running from the English to the Bristol Channels, its edge to the east of Exeter. 'Not cut off from anywhere I want to be, anyway.'

The stock shots of snow ploughs; a list of emergency telephone numbers; more snow forecast.

The local sky was a brilliant blue, and the ground merely powdered with white. Tamara said, 'Can I take the Landrover? I want to go to Stockwell market.'

'Of course. I'm not going in to the office.'

An MP was calling upon the government to provide more cash for some vote-winning cause. An expert had claimed that the East Germans were cynically duping the West by sending fakes to be shown in the Great Exhibition.

'Have a look out at the market for me, darling, I need a little antique fireguard for the spare bedroom, when

Sandra's here with the children,' Olga Hoyland said.

'And now for the Local News. Reports are coming in that an elderly woman pensioner has been battered to death in her lonely cottage on Dartmoor, and the house ransacked.' Anyone who had noticed unusual activity in the neighbourhood of Stockcross was asked to get in touch with the Stockwell police. In the second such incident this year, thieves had broken into Stockwell Comprehensive school; it was not yet known what was missing.

'You're leaving early, Tamara.'

'I want my pick of the market stalls.'

'What about that message to call someone back in London?'

'I did, last night.' Mr Black had been unavailable again, but Tamara had recorded a detailed progress report onto his machine. Long since she had vowed not to become the type of heroine so popular in fiction, so infuriating in fact, who barged into obvious dangers without telling her friends what she was doing, and without any reason for not telling them. Ogden Nash's 'If she'd told the dicks how she got in that fix I'd be much apter to finish the chapter,' was Tamara's motto in her second profession.

The radio warning about treacherous road surfaces had been as minatory as the gale warning for Portland and Plymouth, but the long-wheel-base Landrover was unaffected by the slippery surface. Tamara parked it, as muddy and battered as any local farmer's, in a field entrance near the comprehensive school, made her way round the back of the building and retrieved the bag from its undisturbed nest in the snow. But there were all the signs of police and publicity at the front, when Tamara drove round.

She pulled up, and said to a young uniformed woman, 'Was there much damage?'

'Only the pane of glass they broke, in the porch there.'

'Might have been someone wanting a night's shelter?'

'They keep the radiators going twenty-four hours in there.'

'It used to be freezing all the time at my school,' Tamara said.

'Mine too.' The two young women smiled at their premature rendering of the 'in my young days' speech.

'I suppose the road's clear into town?' Tamara asked.

'Yes, the worst of the weather was further east. You can't get out of the county.'

The road to the market town led past the turning to Miss Christie's bungalow. It was blocked by a police car, and when Tamara slowed, a constable waved her to go on.

Would Kim Rice have found his way there if Tamara had not first done so? Surely the answer must be yes, but Tamara could not halt the wave of shame and sorrow that swept over her at the thought of Miss Christie's death by telling herself it wasn't her fault. When the 'pensioner battered to death', in that sadly well-worn phrase, became a personality instead of a statistic in one's mind, then no vapid generalisations about the socialisation of the criminal seemed helpful or even sensible. Anyway, Kim Rice was by no stretch of the imagination deprived, disadvantaged, or idle. There could be no excuses for him.

Stockwell was a market town enfolded in the moors, left behind by railway lines and main roads so as to have avoided the improvements of the nineteenth and early twentieth centuries; indeed it had hardly changed from what Artemis and Clementine Bessemer might have seen if they were ever allowed to go there, until a reorganised district council had decided that its lack of modern amenities was a scandal and its ancient roads a danger. The twisting moorland lane that led to it spread into a dual carriageway at the outskirts of the town, where there were numerous boards advertising vacant advance factories on a modern industrial estate. Developments of bungalows and Georgian-style houses were creeping up the enclosing hills. Planning permission had been granted in the hope of providing homes for local newly-married couples, but the local papers regularly reported the purchase of blocks of them by the London boroughs putting their old people literally out to grass. Tamara drove into one of the modern roads and stopped in a turning circle. In one front garden a small boy was making and throwing meagre snowballs. Next door, an old man was scolding him.

Tamara pulled her trophies out and spread them on her lap. She had taken a tin of polish-impregnated wool from the kitchen before coming out, and now she rubbed some gingerly on the inside of the stone-studded metal. A silvery gleam shone through the dull surface. Tamara touched the stones, the silver, the rusty edge of the broken sword. She weighed the crucifix in her hand, and peered at the fragment of wood, no larger than her thumbnail, that was set in crystal and filigree.

This treasure would be put away in another vault while the litigation took its weary course. It might never emerge into sight again, for the owners of the nineteenth-century copy would bitterly resent it if their property were shown up as worthless by the original.

The metal was warming in Tamara's hand, though the stones remained as cold as icicles. This is more, she thought, than a national status symbol. It's more than a symbol of financial value. If my work as an archaeologist, and even a scholar, has any meaning at all, then I have to recognise the significance of this lap-full, even if I can't sense the emotional tug I had half expected. This is what archaeology is all about. Not status, not propaganda, not wealth, but knowledge, continuity, and an understanding

158

of the ancient power of such venerable objects.

Archaeology is often accused of concentrating on things, to the exclusion of what they can tell about people and societies. What else can that science do, without written records? But here was a thing that carried with it a record of its own, and a message legible to those with eyes to read it. It must be *seen*.

The Saturday market in Stockwell opened at ten o'clock. Tamara put the 'finds' back into the scarf, and then into a plastic bag that she found under the driving seat. EAT MORE FRUIT was written on it in green capital letters. She drove on into the town and parked the Landrover in the section reserved for farmers. Another shopping bag, containing a couple of boxes of cat food, was in the Landrover, and with a plastic carrier in each hand Tamara walked past the pens of livestock, where steam rose from the animals into the chilly air, and the paving stones were thick with mud and sludge. Stall-holders were setting out their wares in the main market place. The stalls had recently been refurbished, so that each trestle table was now covered with a pink plastic canopy. The old stone fountain had been moved to make room for the public lavatories, and there was already a queue to use them.

There seemed to be no arrangement of categories: old clothes, new clothes, fallen-off-the-back-of-a-lorry clothes; buttons, books, pottery, sewing thread; sports gear, motoring gear; cheese stall, meat stall, seven graded sizes of eggs; the waving banner of the Peace Movement flew above a red draped table, where Mrs Patel and two other women, surrounded by their children, were laying out their wares. All were encased in layers of anoraks, scarves and knitted hats. Steam billowed from their mouths.

Jeremy Ellice was rummaging through the trays of

159

jumble. Tamara stepped behind a barrow of brooms and buckets to listen.

He said, 'I am really looking for a pot to grow indoor bulbs in.'

'It's a bit late in the year for that, dear,' Mrs Patel told him. 'You'll have to wait until next autumn now.'

'All the same . . .'

'What about this one?' She held out a pottery bowl decorated with random lines.

'Not quite.'

'What exactly were you wanting?' Mrs Patel's attention was distracted by another early customer, who bought a stainless steel toast rack. 'We're not really open yet. It's still only ten to. Assad, can you fetch that box from the back of the car, and Deeba, I need some change, see if Mr Dunwoody can change this note. Now, sir, I'd like to help you, everything we sell helps the cause.'

Jeremy Ellice's hand traced a rough circle in the air. 'Just a bowl, really. Metal, perhaps, with some kind of coloured decoration.'

He obviously did not quite know what a chalice would look like.

'Why don't you come back later? Mrs Fletcher's going to be bringing more boxes, she must have been held up in the snow. There might be something else. Or you could look over there, at Duxford's bric-a-brac.'

Jeremy Ellice mooched away.

Tamara came behind the stall, and said, 'Can I help, Mrs Patel?'

'We can always do with an extra pair of hands, especially with Mrs Fletcher not being here yet. You could arrange these better.'

Miss Christie's bowl was in the middle of the table, lying between a Staffordshire dog and a hand-knitted tea cosy. It was too small to be really useful for bulbs, and

160

could never have held more than a single hyacinth. It looked like dull brass, and the stones set on it were purple, green and dark red. The bowl was dented and misshapen, its rim bending erratically, and the splayed foot was too uneven for it to remain upright.

'That's what I'd call a white elephant,' Mrs Patel said. 'Can't see what you'd do with that.'

'Hideous, don't you think?' another woman said. 'Ought to go for scrap, really.'

'I rather like it,' Tamara said, pulling out her purse. 'What were you asking for it?'

'There won't be many people wanting that! Would ten pence be all right?'

'Can I have these things too?'

'I don't remember them. What is it, a necklace or something? And a toy sword . . . couldn't take more than a pound off you for the lot.'

'I have got a bag,' Tamara said, putting her purchases back into it again.

'That is a help. One thing we're always short of.'

'Can I leave it under here a minute while I look round?'

'Put it in here.'

Jeremy Ellice came face to face with Tamara beside Duxford's bric-a-brac stall.

'You found it!' He reached out his hands for the plastic carrier. 'Can I see?'

'This isn't –'

'Come on, girl, don't give me that. This is a joint venture. Fair's fair, half shares each, but even half shares shouldn't . . .'

'There's no money in this for you, Jeremy.'

'Of course there is money. What do you think I am, a philanthropist or something? I'm a trader, Tamara. Everything has its price.'

161

'Anything I have bought here is mine, not yours. I've acquired title.'

She saw the age-old greed of the treasure seeker on his crumpled face. She had found treasure indeed, she thought.

'Title indeed,' he said derisively.

'That's right,' the woman serving at Duxford's stall interrupted. 'You buy it here, you own it, that's the law.'

Jeremy Ellice held out his hand greedily towards the carrier bag, and Tamara stepped backwards, and into another alley of stalls. She dodged past the hurdles set in the path of a hurrying shopper: children, dogs, groups of acquaintances chatting, groups of hagglers arguing. The empty fruit boxes of the greengrocery stall were piled in the footway, and she heard them tumbling, to a shout of anger from the stall holder, as Jeremy Ellice charged past them less nimbly than she had done. The open space in the centre of the market was taken up by a dozen schoolboys playing Christmas carols on brass instruments, and then it was in among the animals, where slow-moving farmers and doting children were the obstacles. She would lead Jeremy Ellice far away from the Peace Movement's fund-raising stall at Stockwell market. Out onto the moors perhaps, where her four wheel drive vehicle could leave him stuck.

The reigning Prince of Horn and Reiss and Drachensfeld was waiting beside the Landrover, his Saab, designed for winter driving, tidily parked to prevent her backing out. His perfect teeth gleamed in a smile. He said, 'I thought I might find you here. Just as you guessed where to find me yesterday. It seems that we have interests in common.'

'Many of them,' Tamara agreed. She put the carrier casually on the bonnet of the Landrover. 'Which one were you thinking of, in particular?'

'We are both re-checking our sources, as all good researchers should.'

It seemed curious that a man of whom one knew nothing could provide a supreme physical pleasure, when that man, revealed for what he was, caused those same nerves to crawl with revulsion.

What did he really want? Not me, at any rate, Tamara thought coldly.

He came round the end of his car towards her, and at that moment a hand from the concealed other side of the Landrover stretched out to grab the plastic shopping bag.

'I'll have that,' Kim shouted. But Jeremy Ellice was already running with his trophy, dodging around the cattle lorries and tractor trailers.

Kim chased after him, leaping and sliding on the slimy surface with the trained balance of a good skier.

Tamara jumped onto the bonnet of her car, to get a better view. Jeremy Ellice had outpaced Kim, and reached his mini van. He tore open the door and started the engine in rapid motion, jerking backwards and around with hasty jerks, his tyres splashing out sprays of mud and slush. Kim Rice reached the door handle just as Jeremy revved up to drive out of the parking space, and just as a bedraggled dog, following his master towards the coffee stall, ran under the van's wheels. The squeal of brakes and yelps of the wounded animal brought the normal buzz of the market to a sudden silence. Jeremy Ellice and Kim Rice were encircled by a group of slow-moving, angry, Devon farmers who appeared suddenly like any crowd attracted to an accident.

From her vantage point, Tamara could not hear the individual words, but the gesticulations were explicit. The farmers were outraged by the wounding of the dog; or no, its death. One of the men took off his leather jerkin, and laid it over the small corpse.

Kim Rice seemed to be simultaneously commiserating, apologising, and demanding the plastic bag. Jeremy Ellice, half out of the car, was holding onto it with both hands. For a moment the two men looked like children fighting over a toy. Then the bag burst, and a rain of small brown pellets fell to the ground: the dried cat food.

Kim, quicker than his rival to recognise facts, turned away with a gesture of disgust, but one of the farmers, a burly old man in gum boots and a green tweed coat, caught onto his arm. Tamara knew what he would be saying; you have to report it to the police if you run over a dog. 'It wasn't me,' Kim would protest, and the farmer, supported by all his friends, would say, exactly as he would have said to two small boys, that he didn't care whose fault it was, they could both come along with him and explain it to Mummy/the headmaster/the police.

This was not an argument Kim Rice could win; here in Devon, not even one that a Prince of Horn could win. Tamara watched the two men escorted along the pavement. They were going quietly, but several of the local men went with them to make sure they did not change their minds.

Jeremy was not the type to fight. He had made his try for wealth, and would be resigned to not achieving it. Kim Rice would not think it was worth the effort to avoid this immediate confrontation. An apology for the death of the farmer's working dog, a payment in compensation, a beer together in one of the pubs that was open for drinking all day on market day, and it would be over. He was clever enough to have left no finger prints at Miss Christie's bungalow or at the school. Tamara would tell the local police force to suspect him, but she knew already that he would never be convicted or even charged with murder. Like other things, that crime ran in the family.

XXI

More snow was falling on the moor, and in her own car Tamara would probably not have been able to get home. She drove even more cautiously than the weather required, burdened by the responsibility for her freight. She was surprised by her own weariness.

Her father was waiting for her, and behind him, a shadowed figure. 'You have a visitor, Tamara.'

Mr Black came forward, and nodded as though his expectations had been confirmed. 'You got it, I see.'

Tamara's arms tightened around the package.

'Can we see it?' Rob Hoyland said.

'Your father and I are old friends,' Mr Black said.

'You never mentioned it!'

'It was unnecessary.'

'We were in the army together,' Rob Hoyland said. 'Recognised each other at once.'

'Do you mean you've told my father –?'

'Safe as houses, aren't you, Rob?' Mr Black said. His smile looked as artificial as a crocodile's. With great but inexplicable unwillingness, Tamara preceded the two men into the long living room, and knelt to spread her trophies on the low table in front of the fire.

There they lay: the broken sword, the dismembered crown with its separate cross, the battered chalice, and for the first time Tamara felt in her heart what her intellect had already realised. These chunks of rock and metal were indeed treasures. She said, 'They belong to me, you know. I paid for them in an open market. I have acquired a good legal title.'

'There speaks a lawyer's daughter.'

'Stockwell is an ancient market overt,' Rob Hoyland said.

'Treasure takes some people like that,' Mr Black said indifferently. He put his hand out to the sword handle, and Tamara made a sharp movement, quickly arrested, to prevent him touching it. He spoke in the soothing voice a man might use to a baby or an animal. 'It's all right. I won't do it any harm.'

'One can see that it will be beautiful when it's restored,' Rob Hoyland said, brushing his fingers against the linked pieces of the tarnished crown.

'I have the ring,' Mr Black said.

'From Plinlimmon's?' Tamara asked.

'They didn't argue. Patriotic duty, and all that.'

Tamara stared at him, and sat back on her heels, feeling the welcome heat of the open stove on her back. Large gobbets of snow were falling now outside the tall windows, and the brief winter daylight was already fading. She said, 'How did you get here anyway, Mr Black? I thought the west country was cut off?'

'The army were very helpful. When it's a matter of the national interest they usually are.'

'He was landed by a helicopter in the paddock,' Rob Hoyland said. 'The geese had hysterics.'

'The national interest,' Tamara repeated.

Rob Hoyland got up to fetch a vacuum pot of coffee from the sideboard at the other end of the room. He poured a mugful for his daughter, and put it into her hands. 'Come on, Tara. Wind down.'

'Let me explain,' Mr Black said. 'I have already told

166

your father all about this. It concerns the exhibition of treasures from East Germany.'

'In which the nineteenth-century copy of this is included?'

'Was included. All the London news media received the same anonymous statement last night, to the effect that the exhibition included blatant and cynical forgeries.'

'It would be hard to show that the nineteenth-century version was a fake, if the Germans don't allow scientific tests.'

'If the showcase contained it, you would probably be right. But the expert who was taken in before the exhibition opens to the public tomorrow says that it contains a crude copy, which could not conceivably be ancient, and doesn't even have real jewels in it. Stuff out of Christmas crackers, one of them said, stuck together with modern glue. It would not have deceived anyone for a moment.'

'That can't be so. I saw the jeweller's blueprint dated 1917. It was meticulous,' Tamara protested.

'When I tell you that there are also traces of the case having been broken into, and a substitution made . . .'

'I don't understand,' Tamara said, rubbing her eyes. 'Three versions of the treasure? Mind, this is the real one, I know that,' she added.

'You are possessive already,' her father commented.

'Why do you suppose that your friend Kim Rice was looking for what you have here?' Mr Black said.

Tamara blushed fiercely, but her father's eyes did not flicker; there were some details that Mr Black seemed not to have told him, thank goodness.

'For the same reason as Jeremy Ellice wanted it. Presumably, to make money out of.'

'No, the Prince of Horn came to Devon either to make sure that the original treasure had not survived, which is what was supposed until he received Margot Ellice's letter; or, if by any chance it had, to ensure that it did so no longer. He did not want any doubt cast on his authentication of the treasure that had certainly been in Drachenschloss in his father's and grandfather's day, and for which he was to receive the price of authenticated mediaeval regalia backed by his unimpeachable pedigree, and with a millennium's worth of provenance.'

Tamara went quite pale. 'Do you mean he'd have destroyed this?'

'Without hesitation. If any whisper of the existence of this lot got out, his purchaser would not have paid for the set stolen from the museum.'

'And that's why he wanted to steal or destroy the Bessemer papers and Margot's manuscript,' Tamara murmured.

'It must have come as a most disagreeble shock when he got Margot Ellice's letter out of the blue with a photocopy of the part of her work that showed Artemis had stolen the treasure. It had been kept so quiet in the family, probably one of those secrets that is passed to the heir on the deathbed . . .'

'But the previous Prince of Horn killed himself in prison,' Tamara reminded him.

'Which would explain why his son made this elaborate and dishonest plan without having any idea that it could be foiled by the reappearance of the original treasure.'

'And now that it has reappeared,' Tamara said. There was love in her voice. She yearned over the artefacts on the table as though they were a living creature. Rob Hoyland and Tom Black exchanged glances, as Tamara said, 'Won't the whole thing make a marvellous story, when these are put on show?'

'Hardly,' Mr Black said drily. 'On show, yes. The story, no.'

'Why not?'

'My dear girl, this is not like you. Always so quick, so intuitive and intelligent. I don't usually have to explain things to you.'

'Words of one syllable, please,' Tamara said, staring at him.

'The East German exhibition is of great political importance. It is the first such gesture made by that régime since its establishment. The first whisper of any softening in their attitude. The exhibition is a piece of propaganda. No more, no less, but one to which HMG attaches much importance.'

'You told me all that before.'

'Then you should be able to see for yourself what effect there would be on the new relationship, if the western media accused the Germans of foisting a modern trinket on us in place of Charlemagne's regalia, and if the Germans accused us of replacing the genuine treasure with that trinket, or of being so careless that we let thieves get away with it. Disaster, either way.'

'Well, where's the first copy?'

'It would have been out of the country within two hours of being lifted.'

'But Kim is down here. He can't have driven out of the west country.'

'My dear, you're being uncharacteristically dense. Kim isn't a thief himself. It was not he who worked as a security guard in the museum so as to be trusted to guard the German treasure. He didn't disconnect the alarms and replace one set of exhibits with another – not with his own hands. That's a very complicated and expensive type of operation. He's one of a syndicate; and he was probably included only because his personal authentication of the goods would raise the price for them.'

'Are you telling me that the exhibit will have

169

disappeared into one of those secret collectors' vaults that nobody can be sure exists? It sounds like story-book stuff!'

Neither man replied. They sat passively in the glooming daylight, waiting for the message to sink home into Tamara's mind. She realised that they were being careful with her, that she was being treated with purposeful tact, like a child, or an invalid, or – a woman. All the same, she needed a few minutes to collect herself. What was that Mr Black had said? She was always so quick, intuitive and intelligent? What was he waiting for her to deduce without being told. She said, 'I suppose you want to put the real treasure, my treasure, into the case. To make a present of it to the German Democratic Republic.'

The firelight flickered on the jewels. One could imagine the ghostly head of a man within that circlet which conferred and indicated his power. What had he derived from the fragment of wood, perhaps two thousand years old, supposedly endowing him with supernatural authority? Tamara put her finger on the crystal. How could a twentieth-century sceptic know what power had once flowed from these inanimate things? Or whether the very conviction of potency created it? Could peace depend on this assembly of stones and metals?

'It's only a trinket, after all,' Rob Hoyland said.

'Trinkets have been the pivot of international relations before now,' Mr Black said.

Tamara said, 'What about Kim Rice, Mr Black? Will you leave him to profit from theft and murder?'

'We shall deal with Kim Rice,' Mr Black said, the promise all the more sinister for his unemphatic manner.

'I don't want him to be dealt with, as you put it,' Tamara said. 'I want him to be tried. I want him to be named at the coroner's inquest. Papa, surely you –'

'I,' said Rob Hoyland, 'want a drink. And you could do

with one. Bring a tray through, Tara, would you?'

The drinks were kept in a glass-fronted dresser in the kitchen. Automatically Tamara set out glasses and bottles, filled the vacuum bucket with ice, poured a package of salted almonds into a bowl. She refilled the ice tray with water and stood holding it vacantly for a long moment, before pulling herself together and replacing it in the freezing compartment. Did she have to give the Germans the treasure? Had she no right to her own political judgement, that it was a régime to which she would give nothing, not even her own hard currency as a tourist? I won't. I'm damned if I will, she thought, and lifted the tray to carry it through.

In the living room the long French windows leading into the garden were open with a blast of cold air coming through them, and the sound of a powerful engine: a helicopter. The curtains billowed into the room, knocking some books off a table, and then were sucked outwards as the machine rose into the sky. Rob Hoyland straightened the lengths of fabric as he stepped back into the room. He fastened the windows behind him, and exclaimed, rubbing his hands, 'It's Arctic out there. But I think the thaw is coming.'

'Father, how could you –'

'My dear, you'll have to take it from me. You couldn't hang on to those things.'

'But they are mine. You have no right –'

'Technically they are yours. It's a quirk of our law. But this is not a case where legal quibbles will help you. Can you see it ever coming to court?' Pouring out two whiskies, and handing one to his daughter, Rob Hoyland went on with his rational, patriotic, masculine explanation of why he had been right to let his old friend Tom Black take the treasure of Charlemagne back to London.

171

XXII

The invitation announced that decorations would be worn. Tamara had none, but she had inherited a Siberian amethyst from her grandmother, which looked well on a dress she borrowed from a friend in the rag trade. Mr Black, who was entitled to a chest-full of medals. wore his shabby dinner jacket unadorned. He stood beside Tamara to watch the formal opening of the exhibition.

Politicians, socialites and academics moved in their overlapping circles. Thea Crawford, not by any stretch of the imagination a dowdy bluestocking, none the less quoted the comment of an English Ambassadress about the French *elegantes*: 'It is odd that their effect upon me is to crush me with the sense of my inferiority while I am absolutely gasping with the sense of my superiority.'

Sylvester Crawford's shrewd eye moved from Thea to Tamara and back. He said to Mr Black, 'Do you know what she's talking about?'

Mr Black was standing next to the case of prehistoric objects which were interesting but ugly: some faded beads, a pock-marked bone ornament, some crude pottery. He said, 'Some women would look beautiful even in these grave-goods.'

The exhibition was of objects from every period. No traces were now apparent of the frenzied work that had gone into its preparation. The initial unpacking of the heavy metal cases, and the arrangement of their contents, went according to a carefully laid plan, and the museum's director, experienced in the ways of enthusiasts, had even adjusted his timetable to allow the expert from the Victoria and Albert Museum to fall into a trance at the sight of the Meissen porcelain, and for the jewellery specialist to make frequent pauses in the work to shriek and coo: 'Oh, it's too much, I've never seen anything like it, I don't *believe* it.'

An international authority on Carolingian art stood beside the main show case. The strain of the last few days could be seen on his face. He had collapsed when he was shown what the burglars had put in place of the treasure he had admired when it came out of its travelling cocoon. It was feared that he was having a heart attack, but after a rest he had revived sufficiently to denounce the fake. It seemed that the exhibition really did contain 'a cynical deception foisted upon a credulous world for political advantage', in the words of the anonymous message to the press.

The old man still looked fragile, for he had spent the previous night hovering over the conservator, watching six months' work being crammed into a few hours. A handful of people knew that the exhibit now shown was not that which had been brought from East Germany. Very few more knew that there had been a robbery, and they believed that efficient police work had recovered and replaced the stolen goods.

A record number of visitors were expected to come to this exhibition, and the display cases were arranged along aisles to prevent enthusiasts retracing their steps or lingering long enough to hold up the queue behind them. The only lighting was from the spots aimed at the objects on show. The maze of partitions, all lined in dark velvet,

173

led inexorably towards the *pièce de résistance*: the regalia of Charlemagne.

The softly gleaming metal and jewels seemed to float out of mysterious darkness, drawing all eyes, even though their brilliance was less than that of the Royal Lady's aquamarine and diamond tiara, even though their materials separately were worth less than the lady-in-waiting's necklace.

The gold and silver of the individual pieces had been buffed into a high shine. Set into the metal were lumps of the gaudiest stones available to Europeans of the first millennium. Except for the ring, the jewels were uncut; smoothed and polished, their irregular shapes studded the regalia.

I had it and it was mine, Tamara Hoyland thought. Now that the treasure was clean and separated from her by booby-trapped glass, it was hard to credit.

Mr Black was reading the catalogue. 'The coronation of Charles The Great, on Christmas Day in the year eight hundred, was the central event of the Middle Ages and altered the history of the world.'

The Royal Lady had reached the main show-case. 'Goodness,' she said. 'It looks very old.'

'More than a thousand years old, Ma'am. It's the Horn Treasure.'

'I know the Prince of Horn. Is he here tonight?'

The lady-in-waiting leaned forward to whisper a reminder. A darker flush spread over the royal cheeks.

'Remanded in custody at a special court,' Mr Black murmured to Tamara.

'In Stockwell?'

'In Hampstead. He was charged with the murder of Margot Ellice. He was seen leaving the house on the afternoon of the fire.'

The Museum Director read aloud to the Royal Lady

the contemporary account that had been reprinted in the catalogue. 'On the most holy day of the Lord's birth, when the King, at mass before the confession of St Peter, rose up from prayer, Pope Leo placed on his head a crown, and he was acclaimed by the whole populace of Rome: "To Charles, Augustus, crowned by God the great and peaceful Emperor of the Romans, life and victory".'

'What about Miss Christie?' Tamara asked.

Mr Black replied, 'One life sentence will do.'

Life; the Royal Lady was pregnant. Forgetting the watching eyes for a moment, she rubbed the small of her back with her white-gloved hand.

Life and victory; the concrete-shouldered men who stood near her, in formal expression of a new relationship between their country and hers, were the victors. They would take the royal insignia of Charles the Great home with them, never knowing that an American collector had a good copy of it, and the Black Museum at Scotland Yard a bad one.

'Crowned by God the great and peaceful Emperor,' Tamara repeated.

'Greatness and peace are both symbolised and promoted by cultural exchange,' Mr Black told her.

'The treasure was on the stall of the Peace Movement in Stockwell market, Mr Black,' Tamara said. 'Somebody owes me one pound.'

DATE DUE

Nº 4 - IMP. DU MAIL 33306

28 JUIL. 1988   5 MAI 1989   26 DEC.

2 SEP. 1988   20 JUIN 1989   07 OCT. 2003

25 SEPT. 1988   22 JUIL. 1989

oct. 26   2 AOUT 1989

22 NOV 1986   16 MARS 1990

22 NOV 1986   7 JUIN 1990   14 JUN 2005

                  03 AVR. 1991   13 MAI 2008

8 AVRIL 1987   0 2 AOUT 1991

27 JUIN 1987   2 8 AOUT 1991

31 OCT. 1987   0 3 JAN. 1995

                 0 2 AVR. 1996

28 OCT. 1988

26 NOV. 1988

26 DEC. 1988   1 5 MAI 2003